PLANET JANET
IN ORBIT

Dyan Sheldon

CANDLEWICK PRESS
CAMBRIDGE, MASSACHUSETTS

Copyright © 2004 by Dyan Sheldon

First U.S. edition 2005

Library of Congress Cataloging-in-Publication Data is available.

Library of Congress Catalog Card Number 2005050789

ISBN 0-7636-2755-0

2 4 6 8 10 9 7 5 3 1

Printed in the United States of America

This book was typeset in M Joanna.

Candlewick Press
2067 Massachusetts Avenue
Cambridge, Massachusetts 02140

visit us at www.candlewick.com

For Chiqui D

FRIDAY 13 JULY

Let the bells of **FREEDOM** ring! The last day of school
finally arrived! As you know, it's been a **GRUELING**
year of hard work and personal development (with all the
stress and slog of GCSEs), but though I'm pleased with how
much I've grown and matured, I'm also très glad it's over.
A person can only take so much graft and growth, and then
she really needs to **RELAX**. So it was all tears and hugs
at the institution today. Farewell, dear friends. See you in
September. Though we won't see **EVERYONE**, of course.
Siranee, Alice, and Sara Dancer are all going to different

colleges in the autumn. It seems like only yesterday that we were nervous Year 7s who thought taking the laces out of our trainers was *très* cool and were awed by the sight of kids smoking behind the science building, and now it was the last time we'd ever walk through those gates together unless in memory. [Note to self: Youth really does go **QUICKLY**, doesn't it?] Because my father is **OBSESSED** with Bob Dylan, I know all of his *billions* of songs by heart, and it's just like he says: Everything passes and changes. Ms. Staples said she was **V IMPRESSED** with my efforts this year and that I deserve to have some fun (at least **SOMEONE** appreciates me!). She said I was going to have to work even harder next year, but she was looking forward to having me for A-level English. I said likewise. I said I didn't know how I could have got through this year without her *Support, Inspiration, and Encouragement*. She said hearing something like that makes working sixty hours a week for a fraction of the salary of a spin doctor worth it. She said I should write to the Prime Minister and tell him, since he seems to think education is only about test results.

Disha's father has pretty much recovered from the trauma of the 𝕹𝖎𝖌𝖍𝖙 𝖔𝖋 𝖙𝖍𝖊 𝕾𝖒𝖔𝖐𝖊 𝕬𝖑𝖆𝖗𝖒, so I'm invited to go to

Greece with her family in August! They're renting a house on some idyllic island untouched by time (except that there's electricity, etc.). I said I thought it sounded terminally **COOL**. After all, **GREECE** is the cradle of Western Civilization. Disha said we'll be on a beach, not in Athens, and anyway, she doesn't think Greece is civilization's cradle—it's more like the nursery. I said so Rome's the cradle, but they're pretty close to each other, aren't they? And she said actually it's Iraq that is the cradle of Western Civilization—from when it was called Mesopotamia. Neither of us is sure how a beach holiday fits in with the Dark Phase, so we've agreed to take a short (and much-deserved) break. After all, even God rested on the seventh day. We'll continue to think **DEEPLY** and be creative, of course, but we're going to forget about jazz and Albert Camus for a while and **ENJOY** ourselves. (To tell you the **TRUTH**, I never finished *The Outsider*, even though it's pretty short, and I always lose track of what the song is in jazz unless there are words.) Disha said we should look on this as **ANOTHER BIG STEP ON THE LADDER OF LIFE**. She said she thought it could be a v broadening experience. Apparently there was a story in the paper about a teenager who fell in love with a waiter at the hotel where she went on holiday and then ran away from home to go back and marry him. (Disha's always reading newspapers. I don't usually bother because everyone knows that they never tell you the truth, and if there's one thing the Dark Phase has taught me, it's that there's enough lying in everyday life without looking for MORE!) Disha said what if we fall in love in Greece? I said I didn't reckon either of us was about to fall in love with a waiter.

Not everyone's going away for the summer. Marcus and David are staying in London (poor sods!). Marcus gets to sleep till noon and play video games all night, but David's dad is making him work in China Gardens, his take-away (no gardens, and miles from China Town, never mind Beijing). We all commiserated with him, of course, but— if you ask me—riding around on a scooter isn't exactly slave labor.

SATURDAY 14 JULY

Oh, how I wish Ms. Staples was my mother instead of
Jocelyn Bandry. It just isn't fair. Of course, I know Life isn't
fair (yet another thing the DP has taught me!), but it does
seem to me that my life is more unfair than most. If there
was any justice in this world, Ms. Staples would be my
parent. Ms. Staples has a *Passionate Soul* and a *Questing
Spirit*. She also truly appreciates me (unlike some **BLOOD
RELATIVES** I could mention). Ms. Staples would let me
go to Greece and expand my cultural horizons. She'd say
I **MUST GO**—my *Spiritual Growth* demands it. The
Mad Cow said, "I thought you were getting a summer job."
(It's incredible, isn't it? She can't remember the simplest
thing I asked her to do for me yesterday, but some passing
remark made **MONTHS** ago, she remembers!!!) I said I
didn't recall being date-specific. She said not only can we
not afford for me to go away, but if I don't start earning
some money soon, I'll finally get my chance to see what
Oxfam looks like on the inside—because there'll be **NO
NEW CLOTHES** this autumn! (I ask you, what sort of
mother would let her only daughter go to school in **RAGS**?)
She said anyway, the house is going to feel really empty

with Justin gone and she'd like my company. I said did that mean Justin's finally been arrested? She said it meant Justin was taking some time off to travel, didn't I listen to **ANYTHING** anyone says? I said only the important stuff. Apparently Justin's tired of taking pictures of poor people in London and is going to South America to take pictures of them there. I asked how it is that she has money to send Geek Boy wandering all over the world to bother the peasants but no money to send me to Greece to expand my cultural horizons. She said Justin's paying for the whole thing with the money he got from his photographs. I swear he does this stuff just to **IRK** me!!!

Disha tried to cheer me up over this **CRUSHING BLOW** (as you know, she's very loyal). She said that, personally, she wishes she could stay in London with me. What's the big deal about sitting on a beach all by yourself? I pointed out that she'd be all by herself if she did stay here because **I HAVE TO WORK**. She said I don't have to work **ALL** the time though, do I? I said I would if the MC had her way. It's just as well slavery was abolished or she'd've sold me off years ago. Disha said slavery still exists. I hope no one tells my mother.

6

MONDAY 16 JULY

I GOT A JOB! Can you **BELIEVE IT**?!! (The MC can't.)
And I'm not working in Woolies or anything like that, either.
(Which, of course, was what the MC suggested. Imagination
is **NOT** her strong point—assuming, of course, that she
actually has one.) I was going past this **V TRENDY**
Mexican restaurant in the neighborhood and thinking how
nice it would be to eat there sometime (it's way too sophisticated and upmarket for my family) when I noticed the HELP
WANTED sign in the window. As you know, I'm very out-
going, have megatons of personality and like to help people,
so I reckoned it was the *perfect* job for me. Also, I'd much
rather work in a place where you might bump into an actor
you recognize than somewhere like Woolies—where the
only person I've ever bumped into is the security guard—so
I just went right in. The owner's name is Mr. Saduki (he's
dark and has a mustache, so I reckon he's Mexican even
though I thought they were all named things like Lopez).
I was prepared to lie about having experience (on the
grounds that I've spent **YEARS** putting food on the table
and clearing it away again), but he didn't even ask. All he
wanted to know was when I could start. I said I was available

1

for immediate employment. He said all I had to do was get my uniform together (I supply the white shirt and black skirt or trousers and he throws in the string tie with the silver D— for Durango) and he'd put me on weekday shifts till I learned the ropes. I said I'd have it sorted by tomorrow. He said and no trainers: you have to wear black, low-heeled shoes. Neither black, low-heeled shoes nor white shirts have ever formed part of my essential wardrobe, of course, so I raced home to get some money off the MC to go shopping. Can you believe it? She said she'd **LOAN** me the money, but I have to pay it back out of my wages!!! (There's just no end to this woman's ability to sink to new depths of bad parenting.) I said since she's the one forcing me to work, I'd've thought paying for my uniform was the least she could do. She said no, loaning me the money was the least she could do.

TUESDAY 17 JULY

So now I know where slavery still exists—in **DURANGO**! My feet feel like I loaned them to someone else—someone who's just walked across the Himalayas in too-small shoes (they may **LOOK** comfortable, but, as we all know, appearances can be **EXCRUCIATINGLY** deceptive!). And there's more to this waiting-on-tables lark than you'd think. [Note to self: Don't **EVER** for even one second consider becoming an actor, as they all work as waiters until the big break comes, which is a pretty depressing thought if the big break never turns up!] You not only have to write everything down and fetch it and all; you're meant to do all this v quickly and with a cheery smile (and you can't stop smiling just because you've got a customer with the personality of Margaret Thatcher). And then there are the Kitchen Staff, who, I notice, Mr. Saduki kept pretty quiet about yesterday. There are three of them and they all look like they've got form, probably v recent. Not that this has made them grateful for a chance to go straight and make an honest living. They've all got **MAJOR** attitude problems and do nothing but grumble and snap your head off. It's all pretty strenuous and stressful. Not only are my feet **ABSOLUTELY KILLING** me, but my face aches from smiling so much! Also, the other waiter on my shift comes straight from hell. Her name's **SKY**! (If you ask me, it should be **BOSOM**, since her breasts enter the room at

least a minute before the rest of her!) She's a complete
KNOW-IT-ALL in the Catriona Move-Over-God
Hendley mold. I tried to ignore her, but it was très difficult
since she spent the *entire* day **TELLING ME WHAT TO
DO**. By the time I limped into the Staff Room (otherwise
known as the Broom Cupboard) at the end of my shift to
get my things, I'd decided I wasn't coming back. But God
finally took pity on all my suffering. One of the waiters on
the next shift was in there reading a newspaper (maybe
they're not as big a waste of time as previously believed!).
I thought *My Heart had Died and Gone to Heaven*. My
first thought was: *So this is what humans are meant to look like!*
His name's Ethan and he's Australian (most of what I
know about Australia comes from those beer ads and a
documentary I saw on how badly the Aborigines were
treated, but, of course, I said that I'd always wanted to go
there). He's only just started too, but he's been a waiter for
over a year. He's almost twenty, and looks like he spends a
lot of time outdoors (surfing, etc.). In addition to being so
good-looking, he's practically a walking advert for God:
Ethan's extremely nice, v sophisticated, and staggeringly
mature (it wasn't a tabloid he was reading!). All I can say is
THANK HEAVEN I never made up my mind about

10

getting serious with either Marcus or David!!! Can you imagine the **agony** if I wasn't **FREE**?!! Have decided to give Durango a second chance.

Sappho was looming in the living room when I got home. (And when I say **LOOMING**, I mean it. I've never seen anyone **SO PREGNANT**—she looks like she's carrying triplet elephants.) Sappho wanted to know how I like the Working Life. I said I don't think it's a patch on the Life of Leisure. After that, all she talked about was indigestion and back pain, etc. (all of which are apparently integral parts of pregnancy). It was dead boring so I went to my room to think about Ethan, which is a lot better than thinking about morning sickness!

WEDNESDAY 18 JULY

The only reason I didn't burst into tears and **WALK OUT** when the man who ordered the Chihuahua Chicken yelled at me so much that I knocked his water over (For God's sake—chicken . . . beef . . . what's the difference? They're both full of hormones!) was the thought that I was going to see Ethan again. Even when Miss Bazooms took over, I didn't lose it. Not even when she told the bloke I was NEW and hadn't caught on yet in this très patronizing voice. *You'll see that face again*, I told myself. *Be cool*. . . . God must be feeling a bit guilty about me, because for once this demonstration of maturity and self-discipline was actually REWARDED instead of punished. Ethan was right where I left him yesterday! His smile nearly turned me to mush, but I rallied enough to ask if he was waiting on tables because he wants to be an actor. He said no, he's waiting on tables because he wants to be a waiter. His *Passion* is travel (he's already been to India!), and being a waiter means he can always get a job. I said I'm going to South America after my A-levels, as I believe that experiencing a new culture is worth très more than anything you can get from books, and he agreed. He said South America is his next destination too! He wanted to know where I was planning to go in South America. I know there are quite a few countries down there, but the only ones I could think of at such short notice were Mexico (because I spend half my life filling tiny cups with pickled chilies, etc.) and Colombia. I said Colombia, because Durango is as close to Mexico as I ever want to get! He said he thought that was very brave of me — because of the gorillas. I said I didn't know they had gorillas in South America; I thought they were only in Africa. He thought this was **HYSTERICAL**. By the time he stopped laughing, I'd worked out that he meant *guerrillas* as in soldiers, not gorillas as in large primates (I must've been paying more attention to **HIM** than what he was saying, which is understandable!), so I acted like I'd meant it as a joke. Ethan said that, all kidding aside, he thinks it's important to have a sense of adventure. I totally agreed.

Had to wash my shirt **BY HAND** tonight because I got something red on it (if you ask me, dark **PINK** would be a much better color for our uniforms). I only hope it doesn't rain, since the Mad Cow refused to put on the heating just to dry my shirt, because it's **THE MIDDLE OF JULY**. I bet if it was Justin, she would've cranked it up as high as it would go. Maybe I should've bought more than one shirt. [Note to self: When you have children of your own, don't treat them the way your mother treats you! Be nice to them!]

13

THURSDAY 19 JULY

NEWSFLASH!!! Mr. Saduki isn't Mexican; he's from Pakistan. Of course, this piece of information came from Sky (which is where she acts like she's talking to me from). Trying to be friendly, I asked her if she thought Mr. Saduki brought the blankets and crap he's got on the walls from Mexico with him, and she said did I mean the Mexico that's next to India? Sky said she reckoned Durango's the closest Saduki's ever been to Mexico. She thought it was ABSOLUTELY HILARIOUS that I didn't know he was from Pakistan. I said well, he looks Mexican, and she said he also looks Pakistani and that if I'd ever done any traveling (as *she* has, of course) I'd know that. [Note to self: Discuss with Disha the fact that people from opposite sides of the world can look so alike.]

I live for the end of my *Day of Toil* and my few stolen minutes of *Bliss* with Ethan. If it weren't for him, I wouldn't put up with this crap for a single second!!! (You wouldn't believe how RUDE and SNOTTY a lot of customers are. Today this woman made me take her meal back THREE TIMES!!! It took so long, she could've

14

gone to MEXICO for lunch!) Ethan said he overheard
the blokes in the kitchen talking and he thinks the reason
Mr. Saduki wasn't too bothered about me not having any
experience is because half his staff quit last week and he's
desperate. I said thanks for the compliment and laughed
(which was the first time I'd laughed ALL DAY!). Ethan
said he likes a girl with a sense of humor! Which is ME,
of course. Everybody says I should be a comedian. I said
it's too bad the chef didn't quit. The chef, whose name as
far as I can work out is Gonzo, has already told me off
FIVE TIMES. Ethan said not to take it personally:
chefs are known for being temperamental because of the
stressful, creative nature of their work. I didn't want to
start disagreeing with him before we'd even had one
date, but I don't see what's so stressful or creative about
wrapping some beans up in a pancake. I definitely think
I'm about to *Fall in Love*!!!

Today I got something green on my shirt! [Note to self: If
you ever work in a restaurant again, make sure you choose
a country whose cuisine isn't so colorful. Like Tibet. All
they eat in Tibet is rice.] If I have to wash my shirt out
EVERY NIGHT, it's going to be in shreds by the end

of the month. As soon as I get my wages, I'm back to the West End for more white shirts. I wonder if they have any that are stain-resistant.

FRIDAY 20 JULY

So how was **YOUR** day, Janet? Bloody awful. I wasn't even supposed to be working today but someone was ill, so (out of the goodness of my heart) I said I'd do an extra shift. This was a **MAJOR MISTAKE**. First of all, turns out it's Ethan's day off. I was so **DEVASTATED** I nearly burst into tears. Naturally, since I was so traumatized, Sky was on top form. (There must be a place people like her and Catriona Hendley go to learn how to be a real cow—**NOBODY** could be born that way!) I couldn't fill a salt cellar today without being told I was doing it wrong! Saduki adores Sky, of course. Even if it was possible to look **ANYWHERE** and not notice those breasts, he wouldn't (I'm not even sure he's ever seen her face!). He's just a phoney Mexican. The second reason this day was the bottom of an **abyss of misery** is because I've

16

worked my feet to a pulp for nearly **AN ENTIRE WEEK**—and what do I have to show for it? **ABSOLUTELY NOTHING**. (Well, almost absolutely nothing.) I've got my tips, but they're not exactly what I was expecting. I thought you were meant to earn a fortune waiting on tables, but I don't have enough to buy a single white shirt, never mind anything I **ACTUALLY WANT**!!! Apparently they keep your first week's wages, just in case. I said just in case of what? Saduki said in case I break something. The only thing I'm likely to break in this job is my back or **SOMEBODY**'s neck. Anyway, I got home tonight feeling about as down as you can get without actually falling through the earth. I really could've done with a nice meal and some pleasant company. **DREAM ON**! Of course, I'm all on my own. Since my paternal parent moved in with Nan, the Mad Cow must be bored having no one to argue with, because she's **NEVER** home (even in the summer, she's got her reading group and her yoga and some class that sounds like Pontius Pilate). Also, now that Sigmund's gone, my maternal parent is taking a new interest in her appearance (I don't have the heart to tell her it's way too late). Most women her age go in for plastic surgery (which, in the MC's case, would be **TOTALLY UNDERSTANDABLE**), but she's decided on a permanent diet instead. Which means there's no real food in the house. So I microwaved myself a couple of her diet dinners (they taste all right, but there's not much to them), since even though I'm allowed to eat as much as I want at the restaurant, I wouldn't touch the crap they serve if I was starving. (I actually saw Gonzo making barbecue sauce out of Coca-Cola and tomato ketchup, which was enough to put me off restaurant food for life.)

Rang Disha. She had chicken and homemade chips for supper (at least someone's mother still believes in cooking!). D says the tips'll be better when I start doing night shifts because people drink more and that makes them generous. She couldn't talk long because her father wanted to use the phone and she no longer has a mobe because her mother threw it in the toilet. (Now Mrs. Paski's going through the **BIG M**. It just never ends, does it?)

When I heard Sigmund getting ready to leave the bunker, I went out to say hello. The deal is that he can use the bunker for his clients, but he has to have the Mad Cow's permission to come in the flat. (Usually I avoid him like spots because I'm still pretty pissed off with him for fooling around with Mrs. Kennedy and destroying our unhappy home, but I was **REALLY** desperate for some *Companionship and Sympathy*.) I might as well have gone out on the street and waylaid some total stranger. Sigmund didn't even ask me how my day was or if I had terminal blisters or was on the verge of **EMOTIONAL AND PHYSICAL COLLAPSE** or anything like that (I ask you, how can it be possible that people **PAY** this man for his sensitivity and understanding?!!). He wanted to know if we'd heard from Justin!!! I said **ALREADY**? He's only been gone a few days! Then he talked about himself, of course. Apparently Sigmund moved into his new flat yesterday, so now I can visit him anytime I want. (That's typical, isn't it? I have to wait on strangers hand and foot just to have some spending money, and he's got a flat!) I said the anticipation had been practically **KILLING** me. Could he book me in for my twenty-first birthday? He thought I was joking. Then I asked him if he could lend me a few quid because I **DIDN'T GET PAID**. Dr. Tell-Me-Your-Problems-I'm-Here-to-Help said **NO**. He said he's penniless because of the new flat and giving the MC money. Apparently it's not easy to support two households (pass me the handkerchief!). I said he should've thought of that before he decided he needed two women.

I'm too horrifically fatigued to write another word, so I'm going to bed. Though, with my luck, I'll probably dream about giving the Texas Tacos to the bloke who ordered the Fajita Tijuana and being asked what language I DO speak since it's obviously not English. (I said MEXICAN!)

SATURDAY 21 JULY

D rang this morning to say that the trip to Greece is off! (She's not sure why—she doesn't listen to her parents any more than I listen to mine.) I was v sympathetic, of course, but, to tell you the truth, this piece of news cheered me up no end. Apparently feeling better about your own miseries because of someone else's is pretty common. Sigmund explained it to me once (God knows WHY). It's called *schadenfreude*, which is German and obviously has something

to do with Freud (all of Sigmund's soul-numbing
explanations have to do with Freud!). Disha wanted to
go shopping to cheer herself up. She has to rethink her
summer wardrobe, since she's staying in London (i.e.,
anoraks and umbrellas rather than swimsuits and flip-flops).
I wanted to support my local best friend, of course, but
I didn't really feel like going. (I mean, what was the point?
I for one do not think shopping is a spectator sport.) So I
asked the Mad Cow if she'd let me have some dosh. Since
the MC's a teacher and not a psychotherapist, like Sigmund,
I don't expect her to be kind and understanding—and, as
per usual, she didn't let me down. Apparently she's trying to
pay off her credit cards before she becomes another of the
government's victims of debt. I said what about the money
she gets from Sigmund? Surely some of this is meant to be
for ME—or does she have other children she's supporting
that I don't know about? She said half the stuff on her cards
was FOR me (which can't possibly be true—we all know
it's easier to get the truth out of a politician than money out
of Jocelyn Bandry!!!). Was about to ring D back and say
I was too FATIGUED to go shopping when I had one of
my BRAINWAVES. JUSTIN!!! For the first time in
nearly seventeen years, I was happy he's my brother. My

Parents' Other Child has always been the sort of nerd who saved half his Easter egg till June and then lorded it over his baby sister because she'd finished hers by Easter Monday. This obsessive-compulsive behavior has always IRKED me, but now I reckoned it could be an advantage. Most people blow all they have on their holiday and then have to walk home from the airport, but not the Sharer of the Bandry Gene Pool. I knew there was no way he wouldn't have left some money to come back to. AND I WAS RIGHT. It was in an old brown jar mixed in with his chemicals in his darkroom (the world of international espionage lost the greatest agent since James Bond when I decided to become an artist or a writer or whatever!!!). There was FIVE HUNDRED QUID in it!!! I feel I'm doing him a MAJOR favor. If he doesn't watch out, he's going to end up one of those old men who live in **poverty and squalor** till they die and then the police find a fortune under the pee-stained mattress. And besides, it'll all be back in the jar before he comes home, so what's the difference? I know Karl Marx isn't popular any more, but I'm with him on this one: From each according to his ability; to each according to her need. My need's pretty GINORMOUS right now. Also found Justin's mobe in an old camera bag.

Took that as well for emergencies, since the MC says they'll be **skiing in hell** before I get another one after what happened **LAST TIME**. Disha and I had a great time (I really don't see why anyone would want a hobby like trainspotting when shopping's so rewarding). I got **SIX** new white shirts so I can do them all in the machine at the end of the week, two more black skirts and two more pairs of black trousers (ditto, one laundry), and a bunch of stuff I **DESPERATELY NEEDED**. Ran into Marcus and David. They'd been buying CDs. (I've noticed that though boys may hate shopping the way real humans hate bad hair, they're perfectly willing to do it if they're getting something for themselves. Sappho says men are genetically more self-centered because of not being mothers, though the MC is obviously the **EXCEPTION** to this rule.) They wanted to know why they hadn't heard from me since term ended, and I said because I've become a wage slave, haven't I. Though in my case it's more of a non-wage slave! Marcus said at least David gets paid for delivering chow mein.

I swear you can't turn your back on the Mad Cow for **ONE MINUTE** these days. While I was shopping, Sappho came over, chopped all the MC's hair off and

DYED IT!!! And not blond or black or even what it used to be before it started going gray (mousy brown) like a normal person would. She dyed it **PINK**! I said didn't she think she was a little old for pink hair, and she said you're not old till you're dead. (How some people delude themselves!) Then I said I thought the school had rules about things like that (I've certainly never had a teacher with pink hair!), and she said if I hadn't noticed, it's **SUMMER**. I said how could I notice when I have to **WORK ALL THE TIME**? I reckon the MC's going through her midlife crisis now. D agrees. She says her uncle bought a sports car when he turned fifty. I said being seen in public with an old woman with pink hair is not the same as swanning around in a Jaguar. I wouldn't mind that. Disha said I would if I'd been with her uncle— he backed it out of the showroom and straight into a police van.

The sales assistant I asked about stain-resistant shirts was well sarky. She wanted to know if I'd ever heard of soap and water. I said I just thought that since this is **THE TWENTY-FIRST CENTURY** and scientists can put human ears on mice, one of them might have come up with something more useful, like clothes that stay clean. She said I was in Top Shop not **The Twilight Zone.**

The MC came snooping around my room and noticed my new gear. She wanted to know where I got the money. I said Sigmund gave it to me. She said she thought he was meant to be broke. I said some people are willing to make sacrifices for their children.

I think I'm getting corns. As if I don't suffer enough!

SUNDAY 22 JULY

Disha had to go to a gathering of the clan today and none of the lads were home, so I broke down and went over to see Sigmund's new flat. It's in Kilburn, which, if you ask me, is one of the most depressing areas in London (and not in a **Spiritual Angst** sort of way, in a what's-the-point-of-living sort of way—all cheap shops and **gloom**). Sigmund's flat is in this old, gray building behind the bingo hall (see what I mean?). The intercom doesn't work, the hall smells of damp, and the carpet on the stairs looks like it's been there since World War I. Sigmund's flat is at the top (needless to say, there is no lift). It took him a few minutes to get his breath back after we got up the stairs, and then he gave me the Grand Tour (which isn't going to make Thomas Cook lose any sleep, believe me!). First stop was the hall (about the size of my wardrobe—*sans* the clothes and shoes, of course); next was the bedroom (and **BED ROOM** pretty much sums it up); after that came the sitting room (ditto, an accurate description of what you can do in it); then the kitchen (stand-in, not eat-in); and finally the bathroom (the window's **INSIDE** the shower!). All of the furniture came from Nan's. The only remarkable thing in the entire flat was the pair of gold drop earrings on the shelf in the bathroom, where Sigmund keeps his rubber ducks (unless he's started cross-dressing, they definitely aren't his, so he must already have a new girlfriend!). The entire tour took all of one minute. (It would've been even quicker if Sigmund had remembered the trick to opening the bedroom door.) And there isn't any heating—unless you count the fireplace. He asked me what I thought of the flat and I said I was speechless, which he took as a compliment. Sigmund said he was

lucky to get it at a price he could afford. I said I was
surprised they hadn't given it to him. The GOOD
NEWS is that there's no space for me to stay over.
I wouldn't be surprised if it's got bugs. Sigmund made
me coffee in his new coffeemaker (it was a good thing
I was there or he would've forgotten to put the water
in!!!). My cup was from the Queen's first jubilee and his
was a souvenir from Blackpool (obviously it's not just the
furniture that came from Nan.) The only thing he could
find to eat were two stale chocolate biscuits. I said, FOR
ME? You shouldn't've gone to so much trouble! Sigmund
lit up a fag with his coffee. I said I thought he'd given up
smoking again, and he said that he had but there's no way
he can stick to it when he's under so much stress. I said in
that case maybe he should just admit that he's never going
to quit, since the only people who aren't stressed are dead.

For once the MC was home when I got back. I said
I thought Sigmund had a girlfriend, and she said, "No
change there then." She wanted to know what the flat's
like. I said it's like a squat—only he has to pay rent. She
said he has no one to thank but himself. He made his bed
and now he's got to sleep in it. I said it wasn't really a

bed; it was Nan's old army cot (does this mean Sigmund and his new girlfriend have to DO IT on the table? She must be a lot smaller than Mrs. Kennedy!). All of this made me think. Only a few months ago, Sigmund lived in a flat with central heating and beds and matching dinnerware, and now look at him! He's only one step away from living in a doorway if you ask me.

Disha rang as soon as she got home from the relatives. I told her all about Sigmund and Kilburn and the possibility that he'll end up sleeping in front of Marks and Sparks. D said that's Life, isn't it? You never know what's going to happen next. I said I know that's true in a general sense, but anyone could've told Sigmund what would happen if he got caught fooling around with Mrs. Kennedy like that. Disha said the reason Sigmund didn't think that sleeping with Mrs. Kennedy would destroy his life is because nobody really believes they're going to get caught. She said, Didn't I remember that politician who dared the press to discover him fooling around and then took some blonde he wasn't married to on his boat? She said it was all over the papers. She said it was a bit like me and my gym teacher: I always give the old bag the SAME

EXCUSE for not playing hockey and then I'm surprised when she doesn't believe me. I said I didn't think it was the same thing at all. I said I thought it was much more like people not giving up smoking (as Disha said she could do WHENEVER she wanted!), because even though the cigarette packets are plastered with warnings like **Danger of Death**, they think they're not going to get cancer. Disha said that if I meant her, the only reason she didn't quit was because she hadn't realized how HARD it was going to be. I said I didn't see why not—it's not like she hadn't been TOLD. Sigmund's been giving up since I was in primary school.

MONDAY 23 JULY

Saduki's got me working Mondays now too (I can't refuse or he'll stop asking—also, I've got to put something away so I can put Geek Boy's money back before he returns from the Third World). So it was another day, another dozen enchiladas. The only good thing that happened was that I saw Ethan. I'm happy to tell you that, unlike the phony Mexican and the Borstal Boys in the kitchen, Ethan shows **NO INTEREST WHATSOEVER** in Sky's anatomy. In fact, he shows no interest in Sky **AT ALL**! (Because Sky thinks she's the Sun to everybody else's Planet, she always comes into the Staff Cupboard when we're in there, making a big deal of getting her stuff out of her locker and banging on about how **HARD** she works. But Ethan pretty much ignores her.) Even today when she leaned over him to get something (and practically **SUFFOCATED** the poor bloke in breasts), he kept right on talking to **ME**!

Sigmund was let into the flat tonight because just as he was slouching off to the mean streets of Kilburn, Geek Boy rang up. Usually the male progeny doesn't say more than three words a week, but when he's ringing from **THOUSANDS** of miles away on **SOMEONE ELSE'S** phone bill, he doesn't shut up. Since the MC and Sigmund were fully occupied, I took the opportunity to have a long soak to try and ease my aching muscles. (Must find out what essential oil is good for **Physical Torture**.) The parents were still on the phone when I got out of the bath. Not only that, but they'd opened a **BOTTLE OF**

WINE!!! (In case you think this is normal procedure in the Bandry household, let me assure you that no one **HAS EVER** opened a bottle of wine because they were talking to **ME!**) So, of course, by the time they did finally hang up, they forgot they only communicate in monosyllables now. Sigmund told the MC she was looking **TERRIFIC** (which is **NOT** what he said to me when my hair went red!), and the MC asked him how he was settling into his new flat. Except that they weren't yelling at each other, it was almost like old times—the two of them **IGNORING ME**, as per usual. So I decided to join in the conversation. I asked how Justin liked South America, which seemed like a perfectly reasonable question to me. They both started laughing. I asked what was so funny about that, and the MC said only someone who had totally left the Earth's orbit wouldn't know where her only brother is. I said so long as he's not near me, I don't really care. Apparently he's in Mexico. I said, That was what I said: How does he like South America? Sigmund said Mexico isn't **IN** South America. I said, What did they do, move it? It's **SOUTH OF THE BORDER**, isn't it? The MC said maybe I should've done a GCSE in geography after all. I asked her if she was aware that drinking made her particularly unfunny.

Vacated the premises IMMEDIATELY, of course. Looked Mexico up in my atlas. Unless the lads at *The Times* made a mistake, it looks as though Mexico isn't in South America, after all—even though they do speak Spanish.

I knew the truce couldn't last. They got into one of their screaming bouts and Sigmund left, slamming the door. He didn't even bother saying goodbye to me, although I went all the way to Kilburn to see him yesterday (on the bus!!!). When I came out in search of sustenance, the MC told me what the fight was about (even though I hadn't actually asked). Apparently she wanted some money from him and he said he didn't have any, so she reminded him that he'd just given me a small fortune and he denied it. The MC says you can trust a thief but never a liar. I said that since Sigmund's reputation as a liar has been pretty well established, she couldn't say she hadn't been warned.

TUESDAY 24 JULY

Ethan said he really envies my brother. I said, You mean
because he's related to me? And he laughed and *Gave Me
a Hug*!!! It was THE MOST AMAZING FEELING
I've ever experienced! A trillion stars exploded in my heart!
ELECTRICITY flowed through every cell in my body.
(I'm certain I was GLOWING, but there isn't a mirror
in the Staff Cupboard, of course, so I couldn't check.) Now
I know what people mean when they say they could *Die
Happy*! I wanted him to *Hug Me Forever*!!! I was so
swept away by *Passion* that I sort of bounced off the wall
when he let go, but I don't think he noticed since he was
still all wound up in Mexico. He wanted to know how
long Geek Boy's going to be away, and I said I reckoned
he'd come back when he ran out of poor people to
photograph. Ethan said he could be there YEARS in
that case. Which is the best news I've had in months.

Nan came over tonight. You'd think a person's mother
would be on his side when his marriage breaks up, but not
Nan. She says the day Sigmund moved out of hers was the
happiest she'd been since D-Day. She says she thanks God

33

every night for finally finding Sigmund a place to live. He was driving her nuts. She said she doesn't know how the Mad Cow put up with him for so long.

WEDNESDAY 25 JULY

D met me after work today so she could get a look at Ethan. Ethan got to his feet the instant we stepped through the Cupboard door (he's not just another *Astoundingly Beautiful* face—he's a GENTLEMAN as well, which makes a pleasant change from the teenage Neanderthals we normally associate with). We didn't have much chance for a chat, though, because Sky barged in, and the Cupboard wasn't big enough for the six of us (me, Disha, Ethan, Sky, and Sky's anatomy). Went home with Disha to discuss the situation. D was TOTALLY bowled over by Ethan. She wanted to know if I was CERTAIN he doesn't have a girlfriend, since it's hard to believe someone hasn't snapped him up. I said he hasn't been in London that long. And anyway, he's obviously DISCRIMINATING and wouldn't date someone just because her breasts are the size of a life jacket. D says if he doesn't ask me out soon, I should ask him. I said I'm still a bit **traumatized** from my experience with Elvin. D thinks I'm overreacting. She said that not only does Ethan not know my brother, but my brother's in Mexico, so Ethan can't be flirting with me because he wants to meet Justin. I said that was true, but being older and wiser does make one cautious. D doesn't think that's true. She says all being older and wiser means is you recognize your mistakes faster because you've made them before. Sometimes she's so DEEP, I think she must have had several past lives.

Sigmund was waiting for me like a lion waiting for an antelope when I got home tonight. He wanted to know why I told the MC he gave me money. I said I didn't. I said she must have misunderstood me. So then he wanted to know what I DID say. I said I'd told her I'd borrowed it and she must've thought I meant from him. He said that wasn't the way the MC told the story. I said, Well, you know what she's like: she never really listens, does she?

THURSDAY 26 JULY

I can't see Saduki making it to old age, not with his temper. His blood pressure must be higher than the Post Office Tower. I had **ONE FOOT** through the door today when he started. In case I hadn't noticed, he's running a restaurant not a social club and unless my friends are planning to order a meal, they're **NOT TO COME AROUND**. I said my friends valued their health too much to eat at Durango. It didn't stop there of course. I was tempted to quit on the spot, but then I wouldn't see Ethan again unless I came in as a customer and **THERE'S NO WAY** I'd ever do that.

FRIDAY 27 JULY

This truly is **THE SUMMER OF MY DISCONTENT**!!! You're **NOT GOING TO BELIEVE THIS**! (I can hardly believe it myself.) I said I'd work today because it's pay day. And guess what? The Dorito Bandito (which I feel is an appropriate name since he doesn't come from Mexico any more than Dorito tortilla chips do!!!) not only deducted the cost of the tray of **DIRTY DISHES** I dropped but charged me for his stupid tie **AS WELL**!!! (Sappho's always banging on about the Working Poor, and now I know what she means!) I asked him when he was going to give me some night or weekend shifts so at least I could make some **MEANINGFUL** tips. He said when I stopped mixing up orders and trying to drown the customers. And if you think I got any sympathy for all this from the MC when I got home, you probably believe in Father Christmas. She said **WELCOME TO THE REAL WORLD, JANET**. She reminded me that I still owe her for the first shirt, black trousers, and those torturous shoes. Fortunately she was getting ready to go out. Women the MC's age need at least two hours to prepare for public appearances, so by the time she surfaced from that, she'd forgotten about the dosh, and God knows the sight of her **TOTALLY** shoved it out of my mind. Not only was she wearing **MAKEUP** (she'd better not have used **MINE**!); she was also wearing **ORANGE** combats and a white shirt covered with dragons. She looked like she'd been tattooed! I asked her if she was going to a fancy-dress

party and she said as a matter of fact she had a **DATE**!
I said who with? The strongman from the circus? She said
with the same guy she went out with last week and the
week before. Apparently she's met some bloke at her yoga
class. I said I hoped he was color-blind, since her trousers
clashed with her hair. She said fashion is fascism. I said tell
that to Naomi Campbell.

Talked to D on the mobe till gone midnight and still no
sign of the Mad Cow. And she's always on at **ME** about
being **RESPONSIBLE**. You'd think she'd ring to say
if she's going to be back **REALLY LATE**. I know
there isn't much chance of it in *that* outfit, but what if
I was worried that she'd been hit by a bus? She has **NO
CONSIDERATION** for anyone else. [Note to self: If
I ever do have children, I will always give them the time
and understanding they need and put them first like you're
meant to.]

SATURDAY 28 JULY

No sign of the MC when I got up this morning. For a
change it wasn't raining, so Disha and I went to the park.
Just because we're stuck in the concrete city doesn't mean
we have to be the ONLY people in the world not to have
a tan. We brought beach hats and sunglasses and flip-flops
so we could pretend we were on the white sands of the
Mediterranean. D and I discussed LIFE and things like that
for a while (D said that even though he HUGGED me,
maybe Ethan was just shy about asking me out—after all,
hugging's a natural, accepted thing and even the Queen
hugs people now and then). Then we plugged ourselves
into our Discmen and gave ourselves over to the worship
of the Sun, Giver of Life. I was sort of dozing off a
bit, imagining I was on a deserted beach with a certain
Australian, when something touched my foot. I reckoned it
was a dog. I'm wary of dogs since the time one came over
all cute and friendly and then attached itself TO MY LEG
and got all excited. (It was très EMBARRASSING.) I sat
up to chase the dog away and NEARLY PASSED OUT
with joyous surprise! It wasn't an oversexed spaniel; it was
one of those little dogs that look like gremlins—and with it

was **ETHAN**!!! Apparently the dog belongs to his landlady and he helps her out by taking it for walks. (Didn't I say he was a **GENTLEMAN**?) He said I was looking a little pink, but I assured him that I don't burn. I asked if he remembered Disha and he said how could he forget her? (**CHARMING** or what?) D and I watched the dog (whose name is Fifi even though she's definitely not a poodle) while Ethan went off and got us all ice creams (which is not the sort of thing you really want to be eating when you want to look your best, because it drips, but I couldn't say no!). He hung out with us for **AT LEAST AN HOUR**! It was **TOTALLY INCREDIBLE**. I can't even remember what we talked about, I was so *Hypnotized by Love* (though there could've been a bit of *lust* involved as well since he is **SO GORGEOUS**!!!). He only left because he had to go to work. As soon as he left, Disha started nagging me again to ask him out before someone else gets her hooks into him. I said I'm working on it.

The MC said I should put something on my face because it looked a bit pink. I reminded her that I don't burn. Asked her what time she got in last night and she laughed and said **THIS MORNING**!!! I said I took it that meant she'd had a good time. She said they had a lot to talk about (we all know what **THAT** means!). I said I just hope she practices **SAFE SEX**. She said, Where would I be if she did?

SUNDAY 29 JULY

Woke up to discover that my face looks as though it's been **GRILLED**. Fortunately it only hurts when I smile (which isn't something I do too much round here!). Went straight to the MC to see if she had any magic potions for sunburn. I said it has to be something that works really **FAST** because I've got to go back to **Hell's Kitchen** tomorrow. The MC said she can't guarantee anything, but she gave me something so it won't blister. Thank God it's pissing down so I don't feel tempted to go to the park in case Ethan's walking the mutt again.

Marcus and David asked me and Disha to go to a film with them. Since it meant sitting in the dark most of the time, it didn't matter that my nose makes me look like Father

Christmas is going to ask me to lead his sleigh, so I said yes. (I wore sunglasses so everyone would assume I'd just got back from some incredible holiday.) The film was OK. (They picked it, which is never an indication of Intellectual Content.) Some of us talked about our jobs. David hates his as much as I hate mine. He says I'm wrong about riding a scooter being fun. Apparently it's all whining customers and dicing with death. (Yesterday some crazed motorcycle courier with some sort of vendetta *deliberately* ran him up on the sidewalk!) David said almost every adult he can think of hates their job. [Note to self: Our lives are but a drop in the ocean of time and yet we spend them delivering cold rice and waiting on people who don't leave tips!] David says his uncle used to get really happy when Friday came around but now it just depresses him because it's so close to Monday. [Another note to self: This may be the destiny of most people, but it's not going to be mine!] Had everyone **HYSTERICAL** with my True Stories of Being a Waitress. (Marcus says I should write a book! I may discuss this idea with Ms. Staples—the school magazine could do with a little humor, since it tends to be dominated by the whining poetry of Catriona Hendley.) The MC was out, as per usual, so Disha came back to mine and stayed the night. D said that even though we always have a good time with Marcus and David, after a conversation with Ethan, talking to those two is a bit of a comedown. She said it's like having a gourmet meal one night and a pot noodle the next. I agreed with her, even though I couldn't remember what it was we'd talked about with Ethan (but it was obviously **GOOD**!).

Spent most of the day mucking about with the MC's new collection of makeup, looking for something to make my face look less bright. At least the pain's going.

TUESDAY 31 JULY

Another day that was dreamed up by Satan when he was in a **REALLY BAD** mood. First of all, **EVERYONE** noticed the sunburn. Saduki muttered something about mad dogs and Englishmen, and Sky said I looked a bit like a racoon—only red. Then I had an argument with Gonzo because he said I had the writing of someone who was educationally challenged (he should know!). Then I had an argument with Saduki because he said I was over-filling the salsa bowls (they're not even **BOWLS**—they're thimbles!). **THEN** I leaned over to reach for something and my brand-new shirt ripped down the arm (and it cost nearly twenty quid!). **ALSO**, I didn't even have a nanosecond alone with Ethan today because Sky was stuffed into the Cupboard with us the whole time.

The MC got on the phone after supper and never got off, so I went to my room and rang D on Geek Boy's mobe. D says it might be the bleach that made my shirt tear like that. I said how can something everybody uses all the time be so destructive? D said lots of things are. She said maybe I should go easy on the bleach. But **HOW CAN I**? I'll be buying a new white shirt every other day at this rate. The MC was still nattering away when I came out for a soothing cup of bedtime tea. God knows who she was talking to: the only ones who talk that much are Nan and Sappho (I know it wasn't Nan because neither arthritis nor Jesus was mentioned, and it wasn't Sappho because neither vomit nor pain came up in the conversation).

WEDNESDAY 1 AUGUST

Ethan said he had something he wanted to ask me. But before he could ask it, Miss Bazooms barged in and **THAT ENDED THAT**. D agrees with me that that's practically the same as asking me out. Now I just have to survive the **long and lonely** night and hope he manages to ask me tomorrow. The rain and my *Longing for Love* made me feel thoughtful and melancholy tonight. Decided to start writing some poetry. I reckon poems may be more my thing than stories since you don't have to worry about plot or motivation or continuity or any of that crap. And also, they're much more open to *Inspiration*, which it seems to me is what *Art and Literature* are about. If I wanted to slog my brains out at something that I never got right, I'd be a mathematician. So far I've only got the first line: *How brief is youth and, oh, how filled with pain.* I'm not **TOTALLY** sure what it's about yet, but it was inspired by my feet (which will probably never heal).

THURSDAY 2 AUGUST

Still haven't had a chance to hear what Ethan wants to ask
me (**OH, WHAT COULD IT BE**?!!), so I said all
casual like that we should go for a coffee sometime
when we're not working, so we can actually finish a
conversation. He positively jumped at the chance! He said
what about tomorrow? He said we could meet at that place
by the canal after I get off work. I said I did have plans for
the evening but I could probably squeeze in a quick cup
before. (This isn't true, of course, but I don't want him to
think I'm not popular.) I've decided to act really surprised
when he asks me out—like it never entered my head that
he might be interested in **ME**. Then I'll hesitate and say
maybe it isn't such a great idea and how there are always
articles in magazines about not mixing romance and work.
Then I'll let him persuade me that I'm wrong. I plan to
wait at least a week before I tell him how terrific I think he
is (but I will kiss him on the first date—I don't want to
play too hard to get).

FRIDAY 3 AUGUST

I'm beginning to think that the **ONE** thing you can count on in Life is that nothing is **EVER** going to go the way you want it to. Really. Maybe I should just quit while I'm ahead and become a nun or something. I mean, being a nun isn't really that bad, is it? You get a place to stay and food and a bunch of other nuns to do good deeds with, etc., and you know you're never going to experience **heartbreak and despair** (nuns are married to Jesus, and Nan says He never lets anybody down). Ethan was already at the café when I got there. I acted like I hadn't seen him at first, even though he stood out like a Jaguar in a car park full of Fords. (He looked **INCREDIBLE**! Every female in the place was looking at him, even the ones with lads.) We ordered cappuccinos and chatted about this and that. When I couldn't stand the suspense anymore, I said, "So what did you want to ask me?" About the only thing that went according to my fantasies from that point on was that I acted surprised. **I WAS SURPRISED**. It isn't **ME** he wants to go out with—it's **DISHA**. I couldn't believe it! My best friend? Is he thick or something? Couldn't he tell I fancied him? He wanted to know if she had a boyfriend and also if

I'd ask her if it was all right to ring her. I could've said she did have a boyfriend (someone **INSANELY** jealous with a black belt in karate), but I decided that was v immature. Also—even though I find it **GALLING** that he's sometimes right—Sigmund says that most people are honest only because they're afraid of getting caught, and I was worried Ethan might find out the truth (the way my luck's going, it's practically **INEVITABLE**). Also, Disha Paski, as you know, is the most loyal friend a girl could have, so I know she'll turn him down flat (which he certainly deserves). I said I'd ask her. Ethan said I was a real mate (but not the sort I'd had in mind!). The MC was glued to the telephone from the minute she got home, so, sadly, asking D if Ethan can call her will have to wait until tomorrow (I don't see why I should *pay* to ask her). Decided to take a candlelit bath to cheer myself up. Stayed in the bath so long I was **TOTALLY** shriveled. So now I know what I'm going to look like when I'm an old lady. I just hope I get a boyfriend before then, since I'm obviously not going to after!

SATURDAY 4 AUGUST

Hung out with Disha, David, and Marcus today. Marcus just got his license (he lost a year of school when he was in primary, so he's older than us), so we went for a drive in the country. It started pissing down while we were still stuck in traffic. We got as far as *near* Oxford and then we left the motorway to find a quaint country teashop (the lads had been without food for two whole hours and were starving, of course). The English countryside looks pretty attractive in pictures and old films, but let me tell you, it's different when it's right in your face. Even if we'd had any visibility in the rain, it wouldn't've mattered, because you never knew what was around the next bend (another car, a dog, a cow . . .). After we nearly hit the cow (and it wasn't just me and Disha who screamed), Marcus started going so slow we might as well have walked. We passed quite a few churches (though it could have been just one church, since we seemed to be going in circles) but no quaint country teashops. Disha said it's because the English village is almost dead. Most of them don't even have a post office anymore. I said did the Prime Minister know about this, and she said that preserving the countryside wasn't a priority of his. In the end we went back on the motorway and stopped at a service station for tea (which isn't something I'd recommend to tourists, since they'd think they'd never left the airport). Came home.

Marcus says I should get my license—I'm going to be seventeen on 27 October after all. Marcus says that with all the money I must be earning I could get myself a car to run around in. I said with what I'm making I could hardly afford a bicycle. But it's not a bad idea (driving, not another bloody bicycle).

Couldn't say anything to D about Ethan when we were with the lads, of course, and by the time we got home, it'd gone out of my head completely. Tomorrow is another day (which can be either good news or bad news, can't it?).

Asked the MC if I could have driving lessons for my birthday. She said did I realize that in order to **DRIVE AND SURVIVE**, you had to be able to do more than one thing at a time and occasionally stop talking so you can concentrate? I said I'd never known it to stop her talking. Then she wanted to know if I had any idea how much lessons cost. I said no. She said well, when I paid for them, I'd find out. I don't see why I should **PAY** some stranger to teach me to drive when there are two qualified drivers related to me by blood. The MC is obviously out of the question (not only is she way too highly strung but we can barely cross the road together without an argument!), so I rang Sigmund to ask him to teach me. Once again demonstrating the caring and understanding nature of the professional psychotherapist, Sigmund said **NO**. He said he was still recovering from teaching the MC.

SUNDAY 5 AUGUST

There seems to be no end to the surprises Life has in store for me (I just wish one or two of them were **GOOD**!). Sappho and Mags were coming over for Sunday lunch, and since a real meal (even a vegan one with all the interesting stuff taken out) is something of an event in this house these days, I said I'd be here. Had a **WELL-DESERVED** lie-in and then talked to Disha for a while on the mobe. (Forgot about Ethan again.) By the time I got off the phone, I could hear activity in the kitchen, so I went out to say hello. Mags and Sappho were at the table as expected. But there was a bloke with an apron wrapped around him, stirring something on the cooker—which *wasn't expected*. (He looked like an old folk singer—beard, wire-rimmed glasses, an earring, and one of those ethnic caps that are popular in the Himalayas and places like that.) I didn't think anything of it because, even though they're lesbians, Sappho and Mags know a lot of men, and I assumed they brought him along because he was hungry. (Though I did think someone could've **WARNED ME**! What if I'd come out in my underwear?!!) As soon as the MC saw me, she started shrieking, "Here's Janet!" like she was a talk-show host and I was the guest. She grabbed hold of the pot-stirrer and dragged him away from the cooker. "Janet, this is Robert Hotspur!" I said, "Hi." Sappho laughed and said, "You have no idea who Robert is, do you, Janet?" I said, "How could I? I only just walked into the room!" The MC did her Bridge-About-to-Collapse sigh and said that Robert is the bloke she's been dating! (To him she said, "What'd I tell you about our Janet? She's not in this world." Which I felt was v cheeky!) I maintained my cool and said that (as per usual) no one had told me he was coming. Robert said he and Joss (!!!) felt it was time he got acquainted with everyone (except Nan and Sigmund, of course!). Robert said he'd been looking forward to meeting me. I said and *vice versa*, even though that isn't strictly true since I didn't really know he existed. He said he'd heard a lot about me. I said I hoped it was all good and he said **SOME** of it was. Apparently Robert's a solicitor, but not the sort who makes **TONS OF DOSH** (which is the sort of bloke we could do with in this house, if you ask me!). Robert works for one of those groups that are always trying to save the planet and all the oppressed people who live on it (Greenpeace or Friends of the Earth—something like that). This made lunch a *très* jolly affair since Robert spent most of it banging on about human rights abuses round the world. Sappho (our very own Rebel Queen) couldn't've been more delighted if she'd just found out she was having twins. The MC and Mags were pretty mesmerized too, but I found it *très* boring for something so incredibly depressing. And I was right about the folk singer bit. After lunch he brought out his guitar! I couldn't believe it! He sat there in **OUR KITCHEN** playing and singing some *très* depressing song about a dead hobo. I was still recovering from that when he went on to depressing Bob Dylan songs. (Disha's right about being older but no wiser.

ß

The MC has obviously learned **NOTHING** from her mistakes!) When the rest of them started **SINGING ALONG** (!!!), I said I was really heartbroken to break up the party but Disha was expecting me. Walked right into a bicycle in the hall on my way out. It was plastered with stickers (SAVE THE RAIN FOREST . . . SAVE THE WHALES . . . SAVE ANYTHING YOU CAN GET YOUR HANDS ON, etc.) so I assume Robert has something against cars and public transportation as well as most governments on the planet.

D was surprised to find out my mother has a boyfriend. I said well, how did she think I felt? And Sigmund's going to be well irked when he finds out—the male parent's always wanted to grow a beard, but the MC wouldn't let him. Then I said, "Speaking of boyfriends . . ." and told her about Ethan. Disha was **TOTALLY GOBSMACKED**. She said but she hardly knew him. Also, I was the one with the crush. I said it wasn't really a crush, I just thought he was v attractive. I'm not a jealous person, as you know— and I'm more mature than many people old enough to be my parents—so I said it was fine with me if she wanted to go out with Ethan. I expected her to say no—or at least to argue. She said **REALLY**? I said of course; it wasn't as if we were going out with each other or anything—he's just a mate. And even though he's très attractive, I'd realized that what I thought might be chemistry was just the smallness of the Broom Cupboard. D said, "All right then, give him my number." I said, "Pardon?" She said, "Well, he is gorgeous—and if you don't want him . . ." If you ask me, she could've put up a bit more of a fight.

The MC wanted to know what I thought of Robert. I asked if he ever talked about anything besides man's inhumanity to everything that pokes its head above the ground, and she said of course he did. Apparently he's a very intelligent bloke with many interests. It's too bad songs about dead hobos is one of them, if you ask me.

MONDAY 6 AUGUST

Buskin' Bob was back last night. He banged on all through supper about the **evil** in ordinary things you find around the house. Apparently there are a number of companies **NO ONE** should buy from because they aid and abet repressive regimes, or exploit the poor, or are determined to destroy the planet. It's a surprisingly long list (and I was wearing at least two of them). After supper he and the MC started going through the cupboards to see what she shouldn't buy anymore. Couldn't take it, so I went to my room and rang D. This proved to be a bit boring too, since she was trying to decide what to wear on her date with Ethan (if you ask me, she's jumping the gun a bit—he doesn't even have her number yet!).

TUESDAY 7 AUGUST

The more I think about it, the more I realize that Ethan choosing Disha is the best thing that could have happened. I'm really v lucky. It's an **ENORMOUS** relief to have seen the real Ethan before it was too late. (Look how long it took the MC to see the real Sigmund!) I mean, aside from the lack of chemistry (which everyone knows is **CRUCIAL** to a real relationship), it would never've worked between us. He's not at all artistic or creative, for one thing—which is something that's v important to me.

56

And for another, he doesn't really have an active sense
of humor. He laughs at my jokes, of course (only my
parents don't), but he never really makes any of his own.
And today, instead of being **STUNNED** by his eat-your-
heart-out-Keanu-Reeves good looks, I noticed that he has
hair on his earlobes (how gross is that?). Gave him Disha's
number and by the time I got home, he'd already rung her
and made a date! I reckoned he must've called
on his mobe from the gents', since Saduki **DOES NOT
ALLOW** personal phone calls on the Durango phone. I
said, "It's not v romantic, ringing someone from a urinal,
is it?" Disha said, "Maybe he was standing at the sink."

Discovered a bowl of rotting vegetables on the kitchen
counter tonight, but when I went to throw it in the bin,
instead of thanking me for helping out in the house like
she's always nagging me to do, the MC shouted at me to
put it back where it was! Apparently it's organic waste for
the compost heap. I pointed out that we don't have a
compost heap. She said we do now. I assume that the box
of bottles next to the fridge means we recycle now too.

THURSDAY 9 AUGUST

Went to wash my hair and discovered that my shampoo has been replaced with something with **NETTLES** in it! Went straight to the MC to demand an explanation. She said, Did I realize that my shampoo had animal urine in it? I said that was ridiculous. Who would put piss into something that was basically soap? She said the company that made my shampoo, that's who.

FRIDAY 10 AUGUST

MC out with Buskin' Bob and Disha out with Ethan. Now that I don't even have my few minutes with Ethan to look forward to (I mean really, what's the point? It's not like he's a real mate like David or Marcus), the only conversations I have in the day are about tacos and cutlery shortages and other hot topics in the world of catering.

Invited Sigmund in for a cup of tea before he went home. He wanted to know whose guitar was propped up in the corner (it'll be his natural straw toothbrush that's moved in next!!!). I said Robert's. He said, "I'm Robert." I said, "The other Robert who's intimate with my mother." Sigmund hadn't been told **ANYTHING** about Robert. He wanted to know if the MC was seeing a lot of him, and I said, "Well, that is his guitar. What do you think?" Then, of course, he wanted to know what Robert's like. I said not only is he musical, but he's very intelligent, has a lot of interests, and has dedicated himself to making our planet a better place.

Sappho says my shampoo does have piss in it. Once again I was v sorry I'd brought it up because she was off like a horse at the Derby. She said remember when I was a vegetarian and discovered that McDonald's chicken nuggets had twice as much fat as their hamburgers and that in America they used to put beef additives in their chips? Did I think it was just them? And what about sugar? Did I know how many things I think are savory actually have **SUGAR** in them? I said well, if everybody knows all this stuff, why don't they do something about it? She said it seems to her that's exactly what Buskin' Bob is trying to do.

*   *   *

Went into the kitchen for a cup of tea to take to bed with me while I wrote and remembered that I'd been ordered to **GET ALL THOSE DISHES OUT OF THE SINK**. Really didn't feel up to it—but also didn't feel up to another hysterical scene (the *Power of Love* **DOES NOT** include chilling out hormonally imbalanced women!). Luckily had one of my brilliant ideas. Stuck them all in the broom cupboard and it only took a minute! Sometimes I think Sappho's right and it really is hard to believe that God isn't a woman.

SATURDAY 11 AUGUST

Came out to breakfast this morning to find Buskin' Bob tucking into a bowl of muesli (yes, **REALLY**!). He was dressed (thank God), but he didn't have any shoes on. The MC told me not to look so shocked. I said I wasn't shocked; I was just surprised, since I hadn't been told he was staying over. The MC gave Robert the sort of long-suffering look she used to give Sigmund. I went to the cupboard to get my cereal but there wasn't any. I said

I thought she'd been shopping and she said she's not buying anything made by Nestlé anymore because of the Third World (I didn't ask). She said I could have muesli (what am I—a horse?). I fixed myself some toast (**WHOLEMEAL**!). I could feel Robert watching me while I was waiting for the toaster. He wanted to know what brand my trainers were. Sadly, I made the mistake of telling him. He went on for sixteen minutes (I timed him!) about sweatshops and things of that ilk. When he finally shut up, I said, "Thank God I'm wearing cotton and not fur or we'd be here till lunch." This was another **BIG MISTAKE**. Apparently the other place besides Durango where slaves are still used is in the cotton industry. Thank God, the phone rang in the middle of this fascinating insight into corporate greed. Saved by the bell!!!

It was Disha to tell me about her date. Apparently there has never been such a brilliant night in the history of dating. Ethan's handsome, Ethan's smart, Ethan's kind, Ethan's funny, Ethan's sensitive . . . I asked if he'd hired her to be his press agent and she laughed. I asked if that meant she'd be seeing him again. She said she'd like someone to try and stop her. Apparently he feels the same about her.

They've got another date this afternoon! [Note to self: Ask Sigmund what the opposite of *schadenfreude* is. You know— when you're *not* happy about something good happening to someone else.]

Rang Marcus to see if he wanted to have another go at finding the Last English Village, but he's been banned from using the car. I said, What'd you do, drive into a police van? He got a parking ticket. Apparently his dad **HAS NEVER** had a parking ticket in his life! So Marcus is back on the buses of London until he pays his father back for the fine— which is pretty much like saying he's not going anywhere.

Tonight Sigmund rang to say he's been thinking about me learning to drive and he's decided he'll give me lessons after all. It'll be something we can do together. I joked that the last time we did something together was the father-daughter three-legged race at the school fête when he broke his ankle. He said he reckoned we were both older and wiser now (which, if Disha's right, means that this time it won't take twenty-four hours before he realizes he broke his ankle!).

SUNDAY 12 AUGUST

Disha spent the day with Ethan **AGAIN**. I asked her if this
meant she was in *Love*, and she said she wasn't sure but
whatever it is feels fantastic (not if you have to listen to it,
it doesn't). My morale and energy levels depleted by my
LONG and **TEDIOUS** hours in **Hell's Kitchen**, I gave in
and went to visit Sappho and Mags with the MC (Buskin'
Bob must've been out saving the mongoose or something).
They've both gone so mad about this baby that they've
turned the spare room into a nursery! Which, of course, we
had to examine every centimeter of. (I'd rather be doing the
tour of the Kilburn squat!!!) Then we had to look at every
item of clothing they'd bought for this kid, including the
nappies (how fascinating is that?!!). Has every woman I
know suddenly taken leave of her senses? Sappho dragged
me into the kitchen to help her make the tea. It was a ploy,
of course. What she really wanted was to know what I
thought of Buskin' Bob. I said he seems OK. She said she
and Mags think he's terrific. I said then it's too bad one of
them couldn't have him as a boyfriend. I reckon he'd be
v useful in choosing politically-correct baby gear. Sappho
said I sounded a bit put out. I said **I AM NOT PUT**

OUT, but just because the MC's besotted with the
Corporate Avenger doesn't mean that I have to be. I said one
woman's knight in shining armor is another woman's
repetitive stress syndrome. I was v glad when our visit was
over. Though not for long, of course. Now that I'll be
learning to drive, I feel I should start paying close attention
when someone else is driving. The MC said if I was going
to be a back-seat driver, I could at least sit in the back.
(It's incredible, isn't it? Buskin' Bob tells her what's wrong
with her toothpaste—**A LOT** apparently!—and her
washing-up liquid and she's off buying crap made from
wild herbs, but if I just say one little thing about not paying
enough attention to what's up ahead she goes berserk!)
I turned my attention to the car itself after that—which is
why I noticed we were almost out of petrol. She was totally
humiliated last time she ran out of petrol and called the RAC
for a tow truck because she thought something was wrong
with the car. Since I'd already been told off once for trying
to help, I let her go past two petrol stations before I asked
why she didn't stop. She said she was boycotting Esso.
This had **ROBERT** written all over it, of course, so I
didn't ask for any of the gory details. We drove on. But trust
Buskin' Bob to pick the biggest chain in the universe to

64

boycott! The MC said he didn't choose it, Greenpeace and Friends of the Earth did. I said it didn't seem to me there was any point, since it wasn't going to do any good. She said that's where I was wrong. Many companies, including Nike and McDonald's, have changed their policies because of public pressure. I said, well, I didn't see why she couldn't go to Esso just this once—as it was an **EMERGENCY**. She said I was old enough to understand the importance of principles. Apparently principles, like puppies, are not just for Christmas. You don't just have them when they're convenient. (I never noticed that this bothered her before!) We ran out of petrol at a traffic light about five minutes after it started pissing down. Then—even though it was **ALL HER FAULT**—she made me get out of the car and help her push it to the curb! This is the first time I've been grateful it's a Mini and not a real car.

MONDAY 13 AUGUST

Now when Saduki asks me if I'll work an extra shift, I
automatically say NO. Before, I always said yes because
I wanted him to think I was keen and hardworking so he'd
put me on nights. But now that Ethan and Disha are AN
ITEM, I don't see the point. I hear enough about their
relationship from her without getting it from him too.
Rang D to see if she wanted to do something,
but SURPRISE, SURPRISE she's already doing
something with Super Waiter. [Note to self: I will
NEVER abandon *My Best Friend* for a man. I think
it's v immature.] I said, Didn't she think she should slow
down a bit? I mean, she doesn't want to get really serious
about someone from Australia. What if he goes home? Is
she planning to move there? She said WHY NOT? I can
think of quite a few v good reasons, a lot of which are
poisonous spiders. I reminded her of that advert. I said that
personally I'd think twice about living somewhere that sees
itself as a nation where a man would sleep with his best
friend's wife but not drink his last beer. Then I said,
"What about sex?" She said, "What about it?" I said, "You
know, has he asked you yet?" She said, "I've only been

66

going out with him for a couple of days, for God's sake." I said, "Exactly. But already you're thinking of emigrating." She said I didn't understand!

Went to the V&A with Marcus. He says he likes the V&A because he finds it v inspiring, but if you ask me he likes it because there's no entrance fee. Marcus wanted to know if I'm *absolutely* certain I don't want to go on a proper date sometime. I said I'm positive. I said I value his friendship too much to risk ruining it by exchanging saliva. What I didn't tell him was that Ethan and Disha have opened my eyes (in more ways than one!). Marcus doesn't inspire the feelings in me that Ethan obviously inspires in D. Apparently Ethan makes Disha feel like dancing among the stars. Marcus makes me feel like having a nice cup of tea— and maybe a couple of biscuits.

Nan came over for supper tonight to meet the Eco Balladeer. As per usual, Nan immediately went into Jesus mode. Buskin' Bob didn't blink. He said he reckoned that if Jesus were alive now He'd be a vegetarian, ride a bicycle, not buy anything that isn't fairly traded, boycott all companies that support oppressive regimes, and grow His own vegetables (now who does that remind me of?!!). I expected Nan to argue, like she usually does, but instead she TOTALLY agreed! (I looked out the window to see if the moon had turned blue, but it was raining.) Apparently Nan's joined some new Bible group that sees Jesus as a rebel. Nan said Jesus had a lot to say about wealth and money, etc., and was v anti-materialistic. Robert said all the Great Teachers were like that because they understood what is truly important. (I thought Nan was going to hug him on that one!) Nan said that the more she learns about Christ and His teachings, the more she realizes that it's easier to call yourself a Christian than actually be one. Robert said this was TOO TRUE, and called her Rose! (I didn't even know that was her name. The MC always calls her Mum; Geek Boy and I always call her Nan; and Sigmund calls her either Mother or—when she's not in earshot—the Thirteenth Disciple.) Nan said her Bible group is really opening her eyes to the injustices in the world. Buskin' Bob said that between 30,000 and 35,000 children die every day of preventable poverty-related causes. He said he reckoned that if Jesus came back now, He'd be an anti-globalist. Nan said she didn't know about that but He'd certainly be pissed off.

TUESDAY 14 AUGUST

I was just congratulating myself on finally getting the hang
of this waiter lark (I'd been on **ONE WHOLE HOUR**
and I hadn't mixed up an order, dropped anything, or had
an argument with **ANYONE!**) when Marcus and David
strolled in. (Of all the joints in all the world, right?)
To tell the truth, I was actually glad to see them. But wary.
I sidled up to them in my best professional waiter mode
and asked them what they thought they were doing. David
said they thought they were having lunch. I said not in
Durango they weren't. Marcus said it's a free country.
Not according to Robert and Sappho, it isn't. But I wasn't
about to argue that right then. I said if they gave me
ANY trouble, they'd only live long enough to regret it.
Marcus said they weren't trying to get me fired, they just
thought it would be a bit of a laugh. I gave them the
table way at the back by the kitchen, tucked in behind the
fireplace so Saduki wouldn't see them. David asked me
what I recommended. I said the Thai place across the
road. This made us all laugh. Marcus said there must be
SOMETHING on the menu that was good, and I said

69

that none of the beverages had been known to kill anyone yet. Then David spotted Sky. He said, "She's a bit fit! Are they real?" I said, "What, her feet?" (She has **ENORMOUS** feet as well!) That made us all laugh too. Marcus and David agreed that all the blokes in the kitchen looked like they had rap sheets as long as your arm. David said he hoped none of them had been charged with poisoning, and Marcus said you definitely wouldn't want to send anything back. More laughter. For the first time since I started, I actually enjoyed myself. And they gave me the biggest tip ever! I was feeling almost happy by the end of my shift—but happiness is v fleeting, isn't it? The Dorito Bandito grabbed me as I was leaving. He said what did he tell me about my friends coming by? I said they were eating. He said I'm not meant to **FRATERNIZE**! I took exception to this, of course. If you ask me, the whole deal with being a waiter is that you fraternize. I'm meant to make the customers feel that they're on to a good thing and not suspect that **Satan's chef and his henchmen** have been done for criminal damage. I said that as far as I could work out, I was the person who made people glad they'd come here instead of staying home and cooking for themselves. Saduki wouldn't listen, of course. Blah blah blah. I was practically shaking with the

INJUSTICE of it all. So I QUIT!!! Just like that! I threw his stupid tie at him and said, "In the words of Bart Simpson, I'm outta here!" It was a truly liberating moment. It wasn't until I got home that I wondered if Sappho has had more of an influence on me than I'd thought.

Disha said she was proud of me for lasting as long as I did at Durango. She said Ethan said Saduki makes Captain Bligh look caring and compassionate. I said now that I'm freed from my bondage, we can hang out more, and D said, "Um." I said, "What does that mean? Only if Ethan's abducted by aliens?" D said it's just that she doesn't have that much time to see him, since he works so much, etc. And he gets a bit funny when she suggests hanging out with someone else. I said what do you mean funny? She said YOU KNOW. I said you don't mean JEALOUS? OF ME? She said not really jealous, but she can tell he doesn't like it. He thinks I'm a bit of a flirt!!! If you ask me, she's making it up. She just doesn't want me to think she's the sort of **shallow and superficial** person who dumps her mates the minute she's got a boyfriend (the sort of person she USED TO SAY SHE HATED!!!).

* * *

Nan rang tonight, wanting to know what I thought of Buskin' Bob. I said he's all right. Nan likes him. She said he seemed like a man of principles. I said if he had anymore principles, I reckon he'd have us living in a tree.

THURSDAY 16 AUGUST

The MC wanted to know why I wasn't going to work again today. I said because I didn't feel that the pittance I earned being a servant justified the grueling labor and constant humiliation. She said, "You mean you were fired." I said, "Actually, I quit." I said I felt the Dorito Bandito was hostile and vindictive toward me because I have NORMAL-SIZE breasts. She said, "What about that boy?" I said, "What boy?" She said, "What was his name? Eden? Elijah? Evan?" (Can you believe it? Jocelyn Bandry, who NEVER LISTENS TO A WORD I SAY, remembers some passing mention of Ethan I once made!) I said I didn't know what she was on about. She said she had the impression from the fact that I never stopped talking about him that I fancied him. I asked if she ever got tired of jumping to the wrong conclusion.

Hung out with Disha a bit tonight (since she's **ALWAYS BUSY** in the day either seeing Ethan or waiting to find out if she's going to see him). More insights into his perfectness. (I even got a *detailed* description of what it's like to **KISS** him! Apparently it's like kissing a chocolate mousse. I said I hadn't realized she'd spent so much time kissing puddings.) I'm v happy for D and I've completely lost the little interest I had in Ethan, but to be honest, it really is exhaustingly boring. I mean he's just a lad—it isn't the Second Coming. I'd rather listen to Robert bang on about the **evil** of the pharmaceutical companies (which **IS NOT** one of his shorter lectures) than hear one more thing Ethan said about anything. David phoned to say he knew somebody who was having a barbecue, but Disha didn't want to go in case Ethan got a chance to ring her from the toilet at work. I know I could've lent her the mobe, but I don't see why I should pay for her to tell him how much she misses him because she hasn't seen him in six hours. I didn't want to go to the barbecue without D, since the only person I'd know would be David and I reckoned he'd be off with the other boys playing video games or something. But I didn't want to sit around the house with the MC and Buskin' Bob either, so

I forced myself to go. David wanted to know if Disha was ill or something, since it's rare to see me without her. This isn't true, of course. I go plenty of places without Disha. David said yeah, but they're all toilets. After the barbecue (which didn't actually feature anything COOKED because no one could get the fire going in the rain), we ended up playing Pictionary. I was partners with David. You'd have to be psychic to guess any of his words. One of his drawings looked like a pyramid. I tried pyramid, but that wasn't it. It wasn't a triangle, a tepee, or Mount Everest either. He drew what looked like a head peering over it. I tried Egyptians and Aztecs. I tried blood sacrifice and religion. I tried Peeping Tom. It was a cheese grater. (The head was a biscuit!) After that, I prayed for All Plays so at least I could look at someone else's drawings. We were all laughing so much, it took hours. I said to David that I haven't laughed so much for WEEKS. David said I should hang out with him more, especially now that Disha and I have had the operation and been separated.

FRIDAY 17 AUGUST

Since I'm unemployed, the MC made me do the food
shopping with her. (First she made me help her put the
mountain of bottles in the car so they don't fall all over the
place every time you go near the fridge!) We set off with
the bottles rattling round in the boot, but we didn't go
to the superstore as per usual (where they have a bottle
bank!)—we went to the street market (where they don't
have a bottle bank, of course!). It was like stepping back in
time, all sweat and rotting vegetables. I said, "Don't tell me
you're boycotting supermarkets too." She said, "Yes. The
big chains are squeezing out the small, local shops and
farmers." I said well, that was **PROGRESS**, wasn't it?
We don't make our own soap anymore either. (**NOT
YET AT ANY RATE**!!!) She said *and* their business
methods leave something to be desired. I said I didn't
think they sold diet meals in the market and the MC said
she isn't buying them anymore because Robert doesn't like
the company that makes them either. Also, real food
doesn't make you fat. At this rate we're going to be
growing our own vegetables in the back garden and
brushing our teeth with sand.

SATURDAY 18 AUGUST

Nearly had a heart attack at supper tonight. There was a
SLUG in my salad! Buskin' Bob said that proved the
vegetables we bought at the market were organic and not
grown in a hothouse on chemicals. (Well, **THANK
GOD FOR THAT!**) The MC said that maybe from now
on when she asks me to wash the lettuce, I'll do more than
just wave it toward the tap. Was still recovering from this
when the MC asked how I'd like to go away for a week
before school starts. For one insane moment, I forgot who
I am, who I'm related to, and how God treats me. I was
suffused with *Joy*! I said of course I wanted to go away.
Hadn't I worked my fingers to the bone and my feet to
wood pulp all summer? Didn't I deserve a break?
I **LONGED** to leave the stresses of the city behind for
even a few short days and really relax and enjoy the long
hours of sun! I asked where we were going. The beaches
of Greece? The mountains of Spain? The olive groves of
Italy? The theme parks of America? The answer is: *none
of the above*. The answer is: the isolated Wilds of Wales.
Robert's got a cottage (of course—he probably built it
himself from wood he found in skips!). The MC banged on

about the cottage and how Robert was bringing Marcella and Lucrezia because they really love getting into the country (I didn't know he had dogs. I'm **ASTOUNDED** he hasn't brought them around—he brings eveything else he owns here!), but I wasn't really listening. I was too **DEVASTATED**. I said of course, my going did depend on whether or not I got another job. (I reckon I can get **SOMETHING** even if it only lasts long enough for me to wave them goodbye.) The MC said if I get a job, I can stay with Sappho and Mags while she's away because she doesn't like me being on my own (she doesn't say that when she stays out **ALL NIGHT**, does she?). What a choice—nesting lesbians or the Eco Warrior and his lover! Things just get better and better and better, don't they?

MONDAY 20 AUGUST

Marcus's parents went out last night, so he invited everybody around for a Waiting-for-Your-GCSE-Results party. He reckoned it'd be a hoot to order a takeaway from China Gardens. Disha didn't want to come. I said I thought

Ethan was off with his Aussie mates for the day and she said eating pesticide-free food must be improving my memory. She said she just didn't feel like hanging out. She had a lot to do. I said, Don't tell me you've got to wash your hair, and she laughed. Had a good time even without female support. David was happy to see us. He said usually he's greeted with scowls and mutterings about how he must've come via Norway. David said that if Marcus wants to make some money to pay his parking ticket, he can get him a job with his dad because they're short-handed right now. I said didn't you have to be Chinese to deliver takeaway chow mein and David said Marcus could keep his helmet on.

TUESDAY 21 AUGUST

Have decided to go to Wales after all. I don't think I could survive a week of talking about nothing but heartburn and natural childbirth (I never thought I'd say this, but oh, how I long for the days when Sappho's conversation was all about politics and feminism and what a mess men have

made of the world!). And, anyway, I haven't found a job.
The MC said I might have better luck if I actually looked,
but I pointed out that unless it's around here I probably
wouldn't make enough to cover my bus fare. She said I
could always be an Avon lady. I said yeah, right. I might
as well just end my life now.

WEDNESDAY 22 AUGUST

Sigmund took me out to supper tonight. He said it was
because I'm leaving on Friday and he won't see me for
over seven days, but I'm not fooled. (Not only has he gone
WEEKS without seeing me, but the last time he took
just me out for a meal I was in primary school and we
went to McDonald's.) I reckoned he wanted to chill me
out about my impending GCSE results, which I have to
admit I found rather touching. It isn't like Sigmund to be
so *Empathetic and Sensitive*. And I was RIGHT! It isn't
like him. What he wanted was to pump me for info on
Buskin' Bob. (Adults always have ulterior motives.) To tell
you the truth, I feel a bit ambiguous about this. (Things

really aren't black or white—our minds and hearts are fogged and gray!) On the one hand, Sigmund behaved like a total idiot and pissed everybody off. On the other hand, he is my father—and he doesn't make you feel like you're torturing some innocent child every time you put on your trainers. He said Nan had a lot of good things to say about Robert (which is more than she ever has to say about anyone else—esp. Sigmund!). Sigmund said he was très sorry about what happened with Mrs. Kennedy and all, but he never meant to hurt anyone. [Note to self: Why do people **ALWAYS** says that when the obvious result of their actions is that they hurt someone? It's like dropping 500 megaton bombs on a city and saying you didn't mean to kill any civilians!] Sigmund says that now that he's realized the error of his ways, all he wants is for the Mad Cow to be happy. He should've thought of that before too, if you ask me. I said, Well then, he has nothing to worry about, does he? She's happy as a pig locked in the green-grocer's (**ORGANIC**, of course!). He said he had hoped that he and the MC would get back together in time— once he'd given her some space. I said he did science at university; he should know how Nature hates a vacuum. If you leave any space, something will fill it (in this case

80

an Eco Warrior armed with a guitar). I said and anyway, what about his girlfriend? Sigmund wanted to know what girlfriend that would be—the one who doesn't mind sharing an army cot? I said the one whose earrings were in his bathroom. He said ever since I was little, he's hoped that someday I'd learn to be observant, and now he's got half his wish. Apparently the earrings belong to the MC. He keeps them to remind him of what he's lost!!! If he hadn't looked so serious, I would've laughed. I mean, really. How much more of a reminder does he need than living in Kilburn?

THURSDAY 23 AUGUST

The papers are full of hair-raising stories of **GCSE Stress and Teenage Suicides**, etc., but I was feeling v laid-back about the whole thing until this morning when I woke up at 3 A.M. in a panic attack and couldn't get back to sleep. My predictions were all good, but what if something went horribly wrong (**LIKE IT OFTEN DOES**!)? Would my brilliant future be ruined forever because mine is a

Creative, Artistic Mind that has trouble with quadratic equations? Would all my *Hopes and Dreams* be dashed forever on the rocky shores of French grammar? As you can imagine, the MC was très sympathetic as per usual. She said there was no use worrying about it now. Then, seeing that this didn't exactly **CHEER ME UP**, she said the worst that could happen was I'd have to do some of them again. I said I didn't want to **DO THEM AGAIN**—it was bad enough having to do them the first time. Went to school with Marcus to collect our results. Once the envelope was in my sweating palms, I couldn't open it. Marcus couldn't open his either. So I opened his and he opened mine. Smiles and shrieks of *Teenage Jubilation* all around when we discovered that our young lives hadn't been blighted for evermore! I nearly kissed him I was that excited!

The MC said I don't have to bother packing Justin's mobe as she doesn't reckon it'd work where we're going. I said what made her think I had Geek Boy's mobe and she said call it a wild guess. She spent most of the night phoning the train stations of London trying to get a timetable. The deal is that since Buskin' Bob has to pick something up in

Oxford on his way and the Mini can't go more than a few miles without something falling off it, we're going to take a train to the nearest town with a station and he'll collect us. I said on what, his bike? She said not to be ridiculous. He has a Land Rover. I couldn't've been more surprised if she'd said he had a private jet. Disha's parents have a Land Rover and it's well cool. Am almost beginning to look forward to this holiday, even if I will be out of telecommunication. At last I'll have some truly private time to take stock of myself before the new school term overwhelms me. After all, a lot has happened in a few short weeks (as in my mother's having sex and my best friend's become **Zombie in Love**). And Nature is very conducive to *Thought and Reflection*, isn't she? Must remember to pack lots of candles and incense to get me in the proper mood for *Thought and Reflection*.

FRIDAY 24 AUGUST

Life really is stressful, isn't it? Up, down. Up, down. One minute you're happier than a slug in an organic lettuce patch and the next it's all **gloom and doom** again. Yesterday the world was my oyster and tonight it's back to being a pit of tar. Anyway, just to show how quickly Life can turn on you, I'm writing this **BY CANDLELIGHT**!!! (Thank God I brought them, right?) Apparently Buskin' Bob's cottage does have electricity but **NOT AT THE MOMENT**. What it also doesn't **EVER** have is heat, which is unfortunate if you ask me, since although it's August (a summer month in the rest of Europe!), it's pissing down and freezing cold. (Oh no, we don't want to go to Greece; we want to stay in the sodden British Isles!) So not only am I writing by candlelight but I'm wearing two layers of clothes and am wrapped in a blanket as well. I am totally shattered and exhausted and possibly in a state of clinical shock, but I have to tell someone what happened. Since there's no one around here but sheep (and the MC was right—the mobe doesn't work!), you, Dear Diary, have been chosen. The train journey was a nightmare, of course. We could've got to Greece quicker. We had to wait ages for our connections and half the time they got canceled!!! It was **DARK** by the time we staggered off the train and into the rain. [Note to self: If privatization is such a brilliant idea, why doesn't anything work properly anymore?] There

was only one car in the car park. I said I couldn't believe
Buskin' Bob wasn't here, and the MC said of course he was
here, what'd I call that? I said that didn't look anything like
Mr. Paski's Land Rover and she said that was because
Robert's is a classic (as in the First One Ever Made). I said,
"But there are three people inside!" And the MC said of
course there were three people inside, Robert had Marcella
and Lucrezia with him, didn't he? They aren't dogs.
Apparently Buskin' Bob Hotspur has reproduced!!! I asked
her why she didn't tell me Robert was bringing his
daughters (or even that he had any!), and she said she did.
I said I thought she said Robert was bringing his dogs
(I mean, really, who gives their children names that make
them sound like bottles of wine?). The MC did her sighing
thing. She said Marcella and Lucrezia are the **WHOLE
POINT** of the holiday since he doesn't get to spend as
much time with them as he'd like. I said, And what am I
meant to be? The bloody child-minder? She said of course
not. She reckoned we'd be **COMPANY** for each other.
(If you ask me, it's like putting somebody in jail and
saying, "Well, at least you've got plenty of people to hang
out with.")

*   *   *

So here I am. I haven't actually **SEEN** the cottage because of the lack of light, but I can tell it's really old from the way it leans to one side. (It's hard to understand why anyone would go to a five-star resort when they could come here!) The MC said to stop griping, because everything will look better in the morning. I can only hope that for once in her life she's right.

SATURDAY 25 AUGUST

(SOS from the hut at the end of the universe!)

The MC was wrong, of course. Not only does **NOTHING** look better this morning—it looks **SIGNIFICANTLY WORSE**. I wouldn't even call this a cottage—it's more like a **HUT**. And it's practically vibrating with spiders (which you're not allowed to kill, of course). Also, it's totally filthy. (Apparently Robert doesn't just want to save the whale; he wants to save dirt and cobwebs as well!) I can appreciate the idea of getting back to Nature (it is a common theme in music, literature, and art, after all), but if we got any further back, we'd be in a cave.

The primitive living conditions aren't the **WORST OF IT**, though!! The worst of it are the Hotspur progenies. Exhaustion rendered them pretty quiet last night, but today they're wide awake. If there'd been a crystal ball handy at their births, the parent Hotspurs would have been totally justified in drowning them straight off, if you ask me. I have **NEVER** come across such totally obnoxious children—and you will remember that I am related by blood to Justin Bandry and live next door to Jupiter (who was banned for life from the local swimming pool because he pushed a little girl in when he was only four). Marcella's not even a teenager yet, but she looks older than I do (here is **ABSOLUTE** proof that children are growing up too fast nowadays, just like the magazines say!). She *never* stops talking. Either she's banging on about herself (**ME! ME! ME!** and **I! I! I!**) or she's criticizing everyone else (esp. her father). Lucrezia's nine and totally demented. One minute she's laughing and skipping about like she's been hitting the organic white wine and the next she's transformed herself into the **Monster That Ate Wales**. The only positive thing I can say about Lucrezia is that she's refusing to talk to anyone but her father—and she only shouts at him. (In my humble opinion, Buskin' Bob should spend **LESS** time saving the planet and **MORE** time looking after his children.) I tried to discuss this with the MC but all she'd say was that Marcella's just at that age (I said, "What? **ELEVEN**?") and Lucrezia has problems (which is like saying the army has a couple of guns).

Buskin' Bob and the MC went out to look for birds in the rain. The Hotspurettes wouldn't go. I wouldn't go either, but I didn't get a chance to refuse. It was assumed that I'd stay in the hut with them (child-minder or what?!!). Since there's no TV—even if we had electricity—I went to find a book. Other people leave mysteries and bestsellers in their country homes for imprisoned guests, but not Buskin' Bob. It's all stuff about politics, etc.! Found something called *No Logo*. I thought it might be a novel set in the fashion industry, but it isn't. Apparently it's "a convincing analysis of the superbrand." Started to read it anyway, since it's the only book he has that doesn't give me a headache just seeing the title.

SUNDAY 26 AUGUST

Question: What's **WORSE** than being stuck in the Wilds of Wales in a primitive shack with **NO ELECTRICITY** and two of the most **IRKSOME** children ever born?

Answer: Being stuck in the Wilds of Wales in a primitive shack with **NO ELECTRICITY** and two of the most **IRKSOME** children ever born and having to sit around the fireplace every night singing "Where Have All the Flowers Gone?"!!!

MONDAY 27 AUGUST

Robert's book is actually pretty interesting. It says at one time it cost Nike $5 to make shoes it then sold for at least a hundred. And that's not all!!! It also says that Nike once paid a mega-famous basketball player **$20 MILLION** to advertise their gear—which was more than it paid **ALL** its workers in Indonesia in the same year! That is a bit off, isn't it? This is obviously an example of the injustices Nan

was banging on about. Must ask her if she's read this book.
(It could solve the problem of what to get her for
Christmas. I reckon she's probably got enough candles by
now, and Robert's copy's in pretty good nick. I'm sure
he'll never miss it—not when he's got global warming
and starving Third World farmers and all those political
prisoners to worry about.)

TUESDAY 28 AUGUST

Lucrezia walks in her sleep (**OF COURSE**—how could
I have failed to guess that?!!). After our nightly hootenanny,
the Deadly Duo went to bed and the MC, the Eco Warrior,
and I settled down to play Scrabble. (You can't play games
with Lucrezia because after about two seconds she gets
pissed off and flings the board in the air.) [Note to self:
Just because a person worries about endangered species and
how many trees are being chopped down in the Amazon
doesn't mean he can't be **V COMPETITIVE**.] We were
debating whether or not *bazooms* was a real word when
Lucrezia suddenly marched down the stairs. I knew right

away she was asleep because she wasn't howling about anything. Apparently it's v important not to wake a sleepwalker suddenly (though no one in their right mind would wake Lucrezia whether she was walking or not—let her sleep, it's the only time she isn't making a scene). While Robert took Lucrezia back to bed and the MC made sure all the doors were locked, I took the opportunity to get some decent letters. I feel the least they owe me is winning one lousy game of Scrabble.

WEDNESDAY 29 AUGUST

Woke up in the middle of the night to find Lucrezia Hotspur IN MY BED!!! Not only that, but she had all the blankets and her foot was in my stomach. It's a miracle I didn't wake her up SUDDENLY by screaming with terror (which was only because I can't believe that even a psychopath would find us out here—never mind come out in this rain). Robert said I should move the chest of drawers in front of my door from now on to keep her out. Personally I'm for leaving the front door not only unlocked but WIDE OPEN!

* * *

THANK GOD this week is nearly over! It was another RED-LETTER DAY here at **Camp Despair**. Marcella informed me that my taste in clothes is v passé (she's not even a teenager, for heaven's sake—what does SHE know about style?), and Lucrezia attacked me!!! Really—as in went for me with a sharp instrument! All I said was that I don't like Marmite and she threw a knife at me! I've seen her hit Buskin' Bob (once with a hairbrush and once with a free-range egg!), but I never expected her to go for ME! I said to the MC that they must have obedience schools for children—like the ones they have for dogs—and the Mad Cow said it's not that Lucrezia's badly behaved (!!!), it's that she has a syndrome. I said she should give it back. The MC (or Joss, as she's known here in **Camp Despair**) said it wasn't a joke; poor Lucrezia's v ill. She's on drugs. If you ask me, it's a shame they don't work.

92

THURSDAY 30 AUGUST

Robert **INSISTED** that we go for a walk today (he bribed
us with a pub lunch and all the crisps we could eat—no
matter who made them!). We all got into our anoraks and
wellies, etc., and then Lucrezia remembered that the rain
was going to melt her and threw herself on the floor,
screaming. It took Robert over an hour to convince her that
the acid in the rain wasn't going to turn her into a Slush
Puppy (and who told her there's acid in the rain to begin
with, I wonder?!!), by which time the rest of us had taken
off our anoraks and wellies and pretty much resigned
ourselves to more brown rice for lunch. The pub turned
out to be **MILES** away, and most of them were uphill
and through mud. I was numb from the cold and the wet,
of course, and muscles I'd forgotten I had were screaming
in agony, but unlike the Deadly Duo, I was too depressed to
complain. All I could think of was Disha and Ethan in some
warm, dry place, snogging and telling each other how
wonderful they are. By the time we got to the pub, they'd
already stopped serving lunch! I reckon Robert knew he was
about to have a mutiny on his hands because he bought
whiskies for him and the MC and **COKES** for us. I said,

"Listen! Can you hear that? It's the sound of principles crashing to the ground!" Apparently no one thought I was funny. (I wish I'd asked David or Marcus to come—they would've thought it was hysterical!) All was well for the few minutes it took Lucrezia to decide that her bag of crisps was smaller than everyone else's and throw a major fit. You could tell that the good folk of the Welsh countryside aren't used to this sort of behavior because **EVERYBODY** stopped what they were doing and stared at us. (And they didn't look concerned that some poor little girl was being cruelly tortured by her father—they looked really irked!) Nothing would calm her down, of course. Robert said he'd take her outside while we finished, but the MC said that was ridiculous (it didn't seem ridiculous to me), so we all left. Halfway back to the cottage, Lucrezia started up again because she hadn't finished her Coke. [Note to self: **NEVER EVER HAVE CHILDREN!**]

FRIDAY 31 AUGUST

Buskin' Bob drove us back to London. I'd've preferred to
have taken my chances with the rail service but, as per
usual, wasn't consulted. So I got to bounce around in the
back with the Hotspurettes (it's like riding in a wagon
pulled by mules). Marcella talked the whole way (of
course) and Lucrezia got carsick (**TWICE**!). Then we
broke down. It was lucky someone had a mobile phone
with her—not that anyone thanked me. It took ages for the
RAC man to come. Then we had to stop in Oxford because
that's where Robert's daughters live with their mother the
actress and their stepfather the property developer—in a
mansion (the ex–Mrs. Hotspur obviously **DOES** learn
from her mistakes, unlike some women!). When we finally
rolled up to ours, I nearly kissed the door to our flat, I was
that happy to be home! I said, "Well, at least we won't be
seeing them again too soon," and the MC said, "Not till
next weekend." I said, "We're going **BACK** to Wales?"
She said, "No, Robert's got *the girls* for the weekend, and
I thought it would be nice if they all came **HERE**." She
thought it would be **FUN**!!! I reckon she was an Inquisitor
in a previous life. I said I hoped she didn't think the Borgia

95

Sisters were sleeping in my room. She said of course not. They could kip in Justin's. Isn't that just like Life? A week ago, I thought there was nothing in the world that could make me want My Parents' Other Child back home, and now that *something* is practically moving in with me!!!

SATURDAY 1 SEPTEMBER

Couldn't get Disha last night, so I rang her first thing this morning. Told her I'd really missed her (which was true, but I didn't mention that I'd missed **EVERYONE**—even Nan!). D said she missed me too. She's still in *Love*, but Ethan's working a lot—and he has his own friends and all. I said, **AND YOU DON'T**? I said why didn't she hang out with the lads while I was away—they're always good for a laugh. She said she didn't fancy it on her own. I said you used to. She said so how was your holiday? Do anything exciting? I said not so you'd notice. I said, So do you want to do something today? and she said she was going to Camden Market with Ethan. She said why didn't I come too; then after Ethan went to work, I could spend the night at hers. I said I thought he didn't like me because I'm such a **FLIRT**!!! She said of course he likes me. I'm blowing what she said out of all proportion and taking it out of context. Since Ethan's showing no signs of going back to Australia (or anywhere else) at the moment, I reckon that if I want to see Disha, I'm going to have to get used to seeing her with him, so I said yes.

SUNDAY 2 SEPTEMBER

The way Disha and Ethan hang on to each other, you'd think they're afraid of falling over if they let go. It was like walking around with some alien creature with two heads. And it takes **HOURS** to get through the market like that. I've never thought of Disha as the quiet, retiring type, but today Ethan did most of the talking. Blah blah blah, the restaurant . . . blah blah blah, back home . . . blah blah blah, his travels . . . (He was almost as bad as Marcella!) Whenever I tried to have a conversation with Disha, he'd start hugging her or something equally distracting, so in the end I gave up. Ethan wanted to know if I'd heard from my brother and I said I didn't hear from Justin when we were in the same house, so I didn't expect to hear from him when he's thousands of miles away. He said (**AGAIN**) that he wished he could go to Mexico, and I said I did too. Disha (a girl who has always defended Sappho and her views!) pouted and asked what about her. Ethan laughed (which I reckoned you could pretty much interpret any way you wanted). At last he had to go and get ready for work (talk about **THE LONG GOODBYE**—you'd think they weren't going to see each other for years!) and Disha and I went back to hers. It was like old times after that—at least for a while. After supper D and I locked ourselves in her room with the candles and the incense, and although there was a lot of talk about Ethan, of course, we also managed to discuss *Life, the Universe, and Everything Else* as well. Had Disha in hysterics with my *Tales of Camp Despair*. She said she didn't understand why I'd said I didn't do anything exciting since just being with Lucrezia Hotspur sounded pretty exciting to her. I said only in the way that being in combat is exciting. Disha said maybe Sigmund could tell me what sort of syndrome she has. I asked if she thought we were as self-absorbed as Marcella when we were her

98

age and D said it was possible, but, frankly, I don't think so. Then Disha said I'd better hope the MC and the Eco Warrior don't get really SERIOUS—as in decide to move in together. Then Lucrezia and Marcella would be like my sisters. I said I've already got one sibling I don't want; there's no way I'm taking on two more. I said speaking of getting serious, what about her and God's Gift to the Catering Industry? I said if SEX was in the offing, she'd better make sure it was SAFE because there's been a lot in the mags lately about SEXUALLY TRANSMITTED DISEASES making a big comeback. She said what was I trying to insinuate about Ethan? I said I wasn't trying to insinuate ANYTHING!!! All I meant was that the diseases that used to be so popular amongst prostitutes, sailors, and kings, like syphilis and gonorrhea, are spreading like wildfire (or like syphilis and gonorrhea!). She said sex wasn't an issue yet because the room Ethan rents is right off his landlady's kitchen and they're not likely to do anything with Mrs. Spader cooking and singing along with Capital FM in the next room, are they? All was well till the bewitching hour of midnight, when Ethan rang. I'd never seen Disha move so fast. (Not even that time we thought the house was on fire!) The second she heard the phone, she was off like a fox with a pack of hounds after it. I got into bed and lay down to wait for her to come back. She was gone so long that I fell asleep. I would've slept till the morning if she hadn't woken me up when she got back. I sat bolt upright, I was that startled. I thought maybe the house really was on fire this time. Disha said there was nothing to panic about. She just wanted to tell me that Ethan said he loves her. I said so now can I go back to sleep?

Have been thinking about what Disha said about the Deadly Duo becoming MY relatives. Just the thought makes my blood turn to POLLUTED ICE WATER! How could I be so BLIND? People like my mother have no sense of *True Passion or Adventure*. They crave security and routine—not a white-knuckle ride on the Kayak of Life. Obviously the MC's going to want to replace the rut she was in (married to Sigmund) with another rut (cohabiting with Buskin' Bob) ASAP. And equally obviously, I can't let that happen!!! It's enough that Fate has saddled me with Geek Boy as a brother without adding the Deadly Duo as sisters. (I could leave home, of course—they always need volunteer workers in Africa—but I feel it's important to wait till I've at least decided whether I want to be a writer or an artist, because I'm certainly not going to be able to even think about that if I'm walking sixty miles a day to get drinking water, am I?!!) There's nothing for it—I have to get the MC and Sigmund **BACK TOGETHER**. And très **FAST**!!! I know the MC's still pretty pissed off with him, etc., but they *were* married for a long time—that's got to count for something. And she already knows what a pain he can be. There aren't going to be any surprises like with Buskin' Bob. (Sappho says the reason people put up with politicians who lie to them and cheat on their expenses and take money from big corporations is because they're afraid that the ones who replaced them would be even worse. I reckon it should be the same in marriage. And **DEFINITELY** in the Bandry marriage!!!)

Marcus had everyone around tonight because his parents have thrown caution to the wind and gone away for the weekend. Disha said she had something to do with her parents. She missed a really good laugh. We played Trivial Pursuit, and David (who, I have to admit, has a v interesting and original mind) **ABSOLUTELY** excelled himself! One of his questions was what *craft* (as in **SHIP**) did Neil Armstrong take to the moon. David thought it meant craft as in **HOBBY**! He rejected knitting, woodwork, pottery, and jewelry-making and said **BUTTER-CHURNING**! He reckoned butter-churning was small and portable enough. Marcus wanted to know where David thought the astronauts were going to keep the cow! Game ended due to hysteria!!!

MONDAY 3 SEPTEMBER

Had a word with Sigmund about Lucrezia tonight (partly because I'm curious and partly because I want to start him thinking that everything isn't as perfect between the MC and Buskin' Bob as he believes!). Sigmund said Lucrezia sounded as if she might be *a bit* autistic. (She isn't *a bit* anything, if you ask me—she's totally out of control!) I didn't think girls could be autistic. I said Sappho says that it's men who are autistic, and he said that's not what Sappho meant. What she meant was that some male behavior also happens to be autistic behavior (well, that's what I said!). Sigmund can't say good morning in less than an hour, so you can imagine how he went on about autism, its symptoms and theories (obsessive behavior is one of the signs!). When he finally ran out of steam, I asked if I could spend next weekend at his. He made a big joke of pretending he hadn't heard me right. He wanted to know if I'd lost a bet or something. He said he'd heard I thought Kilburn was located some-where on the bum of the universe and that he lived in a squat (Jocelyn Bandry really has a **BIG MOUTH**). I said I didn't say it *was* a squat, I said it was *like* a squat because it didn't have central heating. I said I just thought it'd be nice if we spent a little quality time together. Since when was that a **CRIME**? He reminded me that he didn't have a spare room or even a sofa. I could tell that my having the cot wasn't really an option, so I said I'd bring my air bed. Just hope I can get **HIM** to blow it up!

Talked to Disha after Sigmund left. Asked her if she had a good time on Sunday. She said she did all her ironing! I said I thought she was going somewhere with the old folks and she said oh, right, there was a change of plan. I said she should've rung—we had a brilliant time at Marcus's. Disha said she didn't think of it. [Note to self: Is *Being in Love* like having a lobotomy?]

more like the Soul Sister of Britney Spears. Since I'd been **WARNED**, I had my book with me. The book says that big companies don't just sell things like shoes or cars anymore. They sell ideas, lifestyles, and attitudes. (That's why cars have names like Renegade and Cherokee and Picasso, etc.—not Henry or George.) It says that whereas a car is just a machine to get you from one place to another, a Renegade is a **STATE OF MIND**. Personally I think the author may be stretching it a bit. Anyway, I was mulling all this over when I heard a truly irritating voice that I recognized immediately. I looked up. Catriona Hendley and Lila were sitting two rows in front of me. I could tell they didn't know I was there because they were having the sort of private, intimate conversation you have on buses full of strangers. Apparently Catriona got more than a tan during the holidays. She got a secret boyfriend as well! Lila was gushing about *How Romantic* it all was. Catriona said her parents would absolutely kill her if they ever found out. I leaned forward, hoping I could find out who the unlucky lad is, but **AT THAT VERY MOMENT** the girl in front of me started talking on her mobe, so all I could hear was **HER** telling her friend she was on a bus, etc. (Some people are **SO** inconsiderate. There really should be a law!)

*   *   *

Told the MC about Disha not buying the orange top.
I should've known that a woman who won't even buy my
favorite ice cream anymore because of her boyfriend
wouldn't be too sympathetic. She said Disha just wants to
please Ethan because she's in love. Then the MC said it was
a good thing I didn't buy the top, because Robert has a lot
to say about Gap. I said Robert has a lot to say about
EVERYTHING!!!

Must get Disha to pump Lila for more information on
Catriona's *Secret Love*!

THURSDAY 6 SEPTEMBER

Got sent to the corner shop for TP this morning. For the
first time I actually noticed the names of the different
brands. One was called **FREEDOM** and another was
FESTIVAL. Made me think about what I was reading
yesterday. Maybe the book has a point after all. I mean,
what do Freedom or Festivals have to do with TP? Why

not just call it Bog Roll or Something to Wipe Your Bum With?

Went to Hampstead Heath with Marcus today. As you know, the Heath holds some bittersweet memories for me because of Elvin—as well as some painful ones because that's where I crashed that stupid bike and nearly tragically ended my young life!—but I don't believe in living in the past. (I mean, what's the point? It's **GONE**.) Marcus wanted to know whatever happened to Disha Paski. I said **WHO**? He wanted to know if we'd had a fight. I said no, what's happened is that Disha's in *Love*. He said here he was thinking she was in quarantine or something, since he's hardly seen her all summer. I said tell me about it. Marcus said, "We're not jealous, are we?" I said of course I wasn't jealous (jealousy is an ignoble emotion, if you ask me). I'm just fed up with being treated like last year's favorite Christmas present. Marcus wanted to know why he hadn't met this bloke. Isn't she meant to introduce him to her mates? To tell you the truth, I hadn't thought of that. I explained that Ethan works a lot, etc. He said the Prime Minister works a lot too, but you can bet his wife's met his friends. Marcus doesn't think it's normal. Sappho was having a cup of ethically correct tea with the MC when I got back. I asked them what they thought about Disha not bringing Ethan around to meet her mates, etc. Sappho wanted to know if I was a wee bit jealous. I said of course I'm not jealous. I just don't think it's **NORMAL**. Flying against all past behavior, the MC actually agreed with me on this one! She doesn't think it's normal either. The MC said she's introduced Buskin' Bob to **EVERYONE** she knows. Sappho finally admitted that we had a point. She said when she started dating Mags, she even introduced her to people she *didn't* know.

FRIDAY 7 SEPTEMBER

The MC wanted to know where I was going with my air bed and my overnight bag. I said I was going to my father's. She *remembered* him, didn't she? She wanted to know when I had been planning to tell her I wasn't going to be around at the weekend. I said I *did* tell her but because she never listens to anything I say, she obviously didn't hear me. Even though you'd think she'd know by now that guilt

doesn't work with me, she said what about Marcella and
Lucrezia? They'd been looking forward to seeing me again.
(Oh, and I THEM!) I said I felt that spending some time
with my father was more important. She said I'd never
shown any interest in spending time with my father before
and I said that he's never lived somewhere else before. Also,
I think he's LONELY. And he isn't getting any younger,
is he? Men his age have a tendency to suddenly drop dead.
How would I feel if Sigmund had a heart attack next week
and I'd missed my last chance to see him because I was
listening to Marcella tell me which of her friends she'd
fallen out with this week? I left très quickly before she
could think of a comeback.

Sigmund took me to see a film tonight and then we picked
up a pizza on the way home. I was going to get him in a
nostalgic mood by reminiscing about all the good times
we had as a family, but I couldn't think of any. So instead
I told him all about our week in the wilderness at Camp
Despair (except for the bits where the Mad Cow and Buskin'
Bob were all lovey-dovey). I've never made him laugh so
much! He asked if Robert REALLY played "Where Have
All the Flowers Gone?" every night? I said did the moon

wax and wane? He said, "Well, your mother likes him."
Since part of this visit is to start sowing the seeds of doubt
about Buskin' Bob's suitability for the MC, I said I didn't
think the Mad Cow's judgement could be totally trusted.
After all, she was V HURT by Sigmund running around
with Mrs. Kennedy like that and she needed to regain her
sense of herself as a woman (I read this in the color
supplement). I said in that state she'd go for any bloke
whose knuckles didn't actually scrape the floor. Sigmund
looked thoughtful at this, but since he'd determined to be
UNDERSTANDING, he said that from what he'd
heard they did seem to get on v well. I said there had been
a couple of shouting matches in the Welsh wilderness.
A spark of Hope shone in his eyes. He said REALLY?
I said yes, really (these were between Marcella and Lucrezia
or between Lucrezia and anybody else, but I didn't see any
reason to mention that).

Sigmund refused to blow up my air bed on the grounds
that a man who's been smoking cigarettes for over thirty
years needs all the breath he can get. I said he should've
thought of that before he started. He said he wishes he had.

SATURDAY 8 SEPTEMBER

I'm having such a good time with the paternal parent that I'm beginning to think it's almost too bad that Sigmund didn't get a two-bedroom flat after all. It's *v Peaceful and Quiet* here behind the bingo hall—though to be honest the West Bank would probably seem pretty *Peaceful and Quiet* without the Hotspurettes. Also, unlike Buskin' Bob, Sigmund is still buying from Proctor & Gamble, Unilever, Coca-Cola, Colgate-Palmolive, Nestlé, etc., so he got all my favorite things in. And tonight he took me to a v cool restaurant (in Kilburn!) where we ate on this little indoor balcony. We played backgammon when we got back to the squat because he hasn't got around to getting a telly yet. Since I had a few hours to spare, I asked Sigmund what he thought about someone not introducing her mates to her new boyfriend and vice versa. Sigmund wanted to know who we were talking about. I said just someone from school. He said you mean Disha? I said yes, otherwise known as **Zombie in Love**. Sigmund wanted to know if perhaps I was a little jealous. I said NO, I just found it distressing the way she was changing because she has a boyfriend—also, I didn't

112

think it was normal to keep him away from everybody else. Sigmund finally admitted that he thought it was a bit off too, especially for someone with Disha's extrovert personality. He had a lot of psychobabble to back him up, of course. Is she afraid that he won't like her friends and think less of her? Is she afraid that he might like her friends more than he likes her and think less of her? Is she **jealous and possessive** and doesn't want to share him because of her own insecurity? None of this sounds like Disha to me. I've never known her to be **jealous** or **possessive**, and she isn't insecure. She may not ooze confidence the way a slug oozes slime (as Catriona Hendley does) but she's v together. Sigmund pointed out that I'd never seen her in this sort of situation before (which is true, of course—she's always been completely sane). Was mulling over Sigmund's words when the truth hit me the way an asteroid hits a planet! Maybe the reason D's keeping Ethan to herself is because she feels guilty—you know, for more or less stealing him away from me. That would make sense. The magazines are right: it definitely helps to discuss things with someone else. I was really glad I had talked to Sigmund—even though he's always wrong.

*   *   *

Catriona Hendley had THE MOST BRILLIANT
HOLIDAY OF ANY HUMAN WHO EVER
LIVED (and, as per usual, was physically incapable of
NOT talking about it). Last summer Catriona and Mummy
and Daddy went to Canada (which, of course, was the most
brilliant holiday ever that year!), but this summer they "did"
Singapore, Malaysia, Fiji, Australia, Hawaii, Bali, etc. I said
what did she "do," bore them to death? Also as per usual,
she ignored this barbed comment and banged on about
where she went and what she did when she got there.
She did yoga on a mountaintop overlooking the ocean.
She went swimming with dolphins. She went sailing and
surfing. She watched the sun set over the rice paddies. She
went topless on the tropical beaches of Kuta. Up until then
everyone had been nodding and wishing she'd hurry up
and finish, but when she said the bit about going topless,
all the boys looked up with genuine interest (AS IF,
right?). She told David that her holiday experience had
given her a fuller understanding of Asian culture. David said
his experience delivering cold rice and prawn crackers had
given him a fuller understanding of Asian culture too.
I noticed she didn't mention anything about a MAJOR

ROMANCE. This must be even more secret than I thought. Catriona Hendley doesn't get so much as a new hair clip without making certain everyone else knows about it. Reminded Disha that she's got a Mission!

TUESDAY 11 SEPTEMBER

Had to go to the library after school to return some books from last term. (What a palaver! Mrs. Higgle actually came into English AFTER ME! Everyone was shocked. I don't think any of us have ever seen her OUTSIDE the library before!) Anyway, when I came out, Catriona was walking towards the main gate with Mr. Plaget. I could tell she was still banging on about rice paddies at sunset because of the glazed look in his eyes. Mr. Plaget saw me and asked if I'd had a good summer. (I reckoned it was a case of Janet to the rescue!) Normally I would've told him I'd had a v crap summer and was excruciatingly grateful to the State for giving me something to do other than work my toes NUMB, but since he was with Catriona I lied and said it was ABSOLUTELY BRILLIANT.

Suggested to Disha that we have a really mega joint party to celebrate our birthdays (she's 22 October and I'm 27 October) since seventeen's practically eighteen (and eighteen's just a step away from twenty-one, so it's something to make a big deal of). Especially if Buskin' Bob is right about the state of the world. If things are as bad as he says, there may not be anything to celebrate by the time we're twenty-one. I also pointed out that it would be a perfect opportunity to introduce Ethan to everybody in a relaxed and casual way. She said he'd probably have to work that weekend. (So as well as being in *Love* she's psychic, since no one actually picked a date!) She said anyway, she just wants to celebrate quietly with Ethan!!! I said hang on, what about me? We always do *something* together. She said not to be like that. I said *like what*? And she said **YOU KNOW** (but I don't, of course!). [Note to self: Isn't it **ASTOUNDING** how small the world gets when your brain's been fried by love?] So I'm having the party on my own. I'm going to invite **EVERYBODY** (even people I loathe, like Catriona Hendley). And since it's so near to Halloween I'm going to make it a fancy-dress party. The MC will only give me a pittance towards it, of course, so I'll have to hit the Justin bank to get everything I'll need. Does a day pass when I don't **THANK GOD** that my brother's gone to Mexico? Only when the Deadly Duo stay over.

WEDNESDAY 12 SEPTEMBER

BIG NEWS at the Institution! The school's been given a whack of lottery money and some of it's going to the school magazine because Mr. Cardogan—the head, otherwise known as Old Woolly Jumper—feels that there should be more to education than textbooks and tests (which is more than the government does!). So now, instead of coming out once a year, it'll come out every **MONTH** like a proper journal. Ms. Staples says this will mean a lot of work and **ENORMOUS** dedication, but she knows that we can do it. We're having a meeting Friday afternoon to plan the layout, etc. Have decided that despite my many academic pressures I'm going to volunteer for either Editor-in-Chief or Fiction Editor. Ms. Staples wanted to know if I'd written any more stories over the holiday and I told her I'd moved into poetry because

119

I feel it's more emotionally direct. She said she can't wait to read some of my poems. Since I haven't exactly written a whole poem yet, I said they're still too rough to show.

THURSDAY 13 SEPTEMBER

Not only has *Love* destroyed Disha Paski's ability to socialize and choose her own clothes, but it's badly affected her investigative skills as well. She didn't get **ANYTHING** out of Lila. She told Lila all about being in love with Ethan and then v casually mentioned that she'd heard Catriona was also in love. Lila wanted to know where she heard that. Disha said around. Lila said it was news to her. This is such **INCREDIBLY UNTYPICAL LILA BEHAVIOR** that I can only assume there is something **REALLY** wrong with this bloke. Disha said maybe Lila was telling the truth and there isn't any bloke. Maybe I mistook what Catriona said. I said there was nothing to mistake in **MUMMY AND DADDY WILL KILL ME IF THEY FIND OUT.** I said since the Hendleys are media people and très liberal

120

and all, I reckon this could mean that he's either **MUCH OLDER** (like over twenty) or even that he's **MARRIED**! Disha said not to get carried away. She said there could be *dozens* of reasons why Catriona doesn't think her parents would approve. I said like what? He's got two heads? He's an arms dealer? He's in prison? She said no—maybe he's a squatter or a protestor or a Womble or an anarchist or something like that. Catriona does like to think of herself as being v cutting edge, doesn't she? I said **A WOMBLE**? A Womble's a fictional character that lives on Wimbledon Common. She said not that kind of Womble, the kind that wears a white boiler suit and goes to all the anti-globalization demos. (I could ask Buskin' Bob for more details on this, of course, but I don't like to encourage him.)

SATURDAY 15 SEPTEMBER

If the truly *Creative Soul* is destined to suffer then I must be the reincarnation of Leonardo da Vinci or someone like that, because I've certainly got the suffering bit down! Wait till you hear what's happened **NOW**!!! We had this **GINORMOUS** meeting yesterday about what sort of magazine we want to have and what we're going to call it and put in it, etc. (We're calling it *Speak Out! The Students' Voice* and we decided that it has to have a popular side as well as a cultural one or it'll just end up underneath budgie poo.) After we decided all that, Ms. Staples wanted to know if anyone was interested in the **∨ DEMANDING** job of Editor-in-Chief. Catriona Hendley's hand shot up like it'd been fired from a missile launcher. Not only did Catriona *want* it, but she'd actually written a statement of Editorial Policy **AND** *jotted down a few ideas* (three pages of them!!!). Ms. Staples said she was impressed by Catriona's organizational skills (being able to put on her makeup **AND** rule the world at the same time) and gave her the job. I could've argued, of course, but I decided to let Catriona have it. I don't want to waste all my precious time **ORGANIZING**, mine is a creative not a managerial spirit, after all. I thought I might take the post of Fiction Editor instead but while I was still mulling it over, Ms. Staples gave it to David! So I volunteered to have my own column (which I reckon is almost as good as being an editor—maybe even better really since you don't have to

122

read a lot of other people's work). I said I'd been thinking of doing a series of humorous articles on working as a waiter, which would give my fellow students a good laugh as well as a vivid idea of what it's like in the world of the Wage Slave (and would make them as happy as I am not to be part of it). Ms. Staples thought it was a brilliant idea but reckoned that it's more a single article than a series. She said she wants me to be the main feature writer. That way I can do timely articles and interviews as well as humorous pieces. I know she meant this as a compliment and all, but being the main feature writer isn't the same as being one of the editors or a regular columnist. I mean, I don't get to make any decisions or tell anybody what to do, I just get to WORK. Ms. Staples said a magazine is NOTHING without good writers. Big deal, right? I mean, the world is nothing without the people who clear the rubbish and sweep the streets, but you never hear about them, do you? All you hear about is the people who boss them around and make all the money. It's the same with history. History's all about kings and queens and generals—not about the people who built the palaces or did all the work in them or actually had their limbs blown off, etc., fighting the wars. I mean, you never see a blue plaque for a cook or a cleaner or the maid who emptied the bedpans, and yet what would've happened without them? (The Royal Family and their friends would've starved to death or died of the stench, that's what would've happened!) I thanked Ms. Staples and said I'd think it over.

SUNDAY 16 SEPTEMBER

Disha stayed over last night. She wasn't here ten minutes when she decided she'd better text Ethan to tell him where she was. I said I thought her mobe had gone in the loo. She just blew all her savings on a new one, as it's **IMPOSSIBLE** to be in *Love* and be tied to a landline. She said just think about it. If Romeo and Juliet had had mobes, they would never have killed themselves. I said it was more likely that they'd never've got together in the first place because she would've been talking all the time. So the girls' night in was periodically disturbed by him texting her or her texting him. Then, as per usual, he rang her at midnight after his shift. After a few hours of listening to them cooing at each other, I asked her to go to the bathroom to talk to him so I could get some sleep. If you ask me, *Love* may be great for the person who's in it, but it sucks for her friends.

This was the first time Disha met Buskin' Bob, of course. She thinks he's rather good-looking. I said and on what planet would that be, precisely? She said no, really. She thinks he's nice. I said that *Love* is obviously eating away at her brain (like syphilis)! [Note to self: Can *Love* be considered a sexually transmitted disease?!!] She said I'm just being defensive, which is understandable since I don't like the idea of some other man replacing my father (which isn't true—I'd be **DELIGHTED** if Harrison Ford replaced him). Disha said at least Buskin' Bob cooks and stuff like that. I said just because he knows how to wash up doesn't mean he doesn't have his **dark** side. Let's not forget that his first wife booted him out. Disha said Sigmund's first wife booted him out too.

MONDAY 17 SEPTEMBER

I think Ms. Staples must've noticed that I was a bit unhappy about not having a fixed position on the mag, because she took me aside after English today. She said she'd been thinking of ways to give the magazine more popular appeal and she thought she'd come up with something. (For one wild moment I thought she was going to dump Catriona, but—sadly—that wasn't it.) She wondered how I'd feel about doing a Personal Advice Column. I said I'd never thought about anything like that because Fiction's my thing, of course. Ms. Staples said that's what makes me PERFECT for the job. She reckons that with my writer's empathy and my sense of humor I'll be able to write a column that gives sound advice and is entertaining at the same time. I admitted that I've DEFINITELY had my share of problems in the last year (and probably someone else's!), so I do have plenty of experience in **suffering and angst**. On the other hand, even though my father's a psychoanalyst, I never really listen to him, so I don't really know the theories, etc. Ms. Staples says that isn't necessary. This is a school magazine not the *Observer*. And she thinks that the people who know all the theories don't necessarily know what goes on with people any more than the rest of us. I said that's v true of my father—most of the time he knows even less. Ms. Staples says all I need to do is be **SENSIBLE**. Which, of course, I always am. The more I think about it, the more the idea appeals to me. After all, I am **EXTREMELY** qualified for the job because of my family and my almost-broken hearts, etc.—and it should be good practice for my mission to bring the MC and Sigmund back together as well! Also, it isn't going to be too strenuous (answering a couple of letters), so it won't interfere with my own *Creative* work. I'm going to call it **HELP!** and my name's going to be Aunt Know-It-All (which is both funny and serious). Ms. Staples said it's v important that I keep my anonymity, so she and I are the only ones who'll know who Aunt Know-It-All really is. I can't even tell Disha! (This would've been a problem a few months ago, but since I hardly see her and the only thing she's interested in is the Wizard, it's as easy as eating a packet of crisps!) Spent most of tonight writing my request for problems. See what you think of this:

Stressed out? Depressed? Picked on? Nagged? Misunderstood? Worried? Insecure? Do your parents ignore you? Your friends take

*you for granted? Your teachers give you a hard time? Do you find
the world difficult to understand? Well, weep no more!* **HELP!**
*has arrived!!! No matter what your problem—be it a lost love or
a few gained pounds—Aunt Know-It-All will show you how to
solve it. Send your questions or even just your general thoughts
about life on our planet to Aunt Know-It-All c/o* **Speak Out!
The Students' Voice**. *Auntie K is here for YOU!*

Since I'm not Catriona Hendley, I don't want to boast, but
I do think it's pretty good. Showed it to the MC (I don't
reckon she counts as telling). *As per usual*, she was as
supportive and encouraging as an attack of fighter jets. She
said TALK ABOUT THE BLIND LEADING THE
BLIND! Personally I thought that was a bit harsh. After
all, even SHE has admitted that I've matured a lot over
the last year (thanks to the Dark Phase and Male Duplicity).
Also I AM a teenager. If you were a teenager, who would
you rather get advice from—ME or someone who can't
even remember what it feels like to be FORTY?

TUESDAY 18 SEPTEMBER

I got to school early this morning so I could run off my
flyers and put them up before classes started. And were all
my efforts rewarded? Is there a pot of gold at the end of
the rainbow? The answer to both those questions is **NO**.
When I went to collect my post this afternoon there wasn't
ONE LETTER for Aunt Know-It-All!!! As accustomed as
I am to the **DISAPPOINTMENTS** of Life, I couldn't
believe it. I really thought I'd have to hire a cab to get
them all home! Ms. Staples said I have to give my potential
readers a chance. Like at least overnight.

The MC was out tonight, as per usual, so I invited
Sigmund in for a cup of tea. After we exhausted the topics
of the weather, school, and his flat, he wanted to know
how everything was going. I said oh, fine, just fine —
quietly and rather sadly as though I wanted to spare him
the really bad news. With the instincts of the professional
psychoanalyst, Sigmund immediately asked me what was
wrong. I said, "Nothing." He said, "You can tell me; I'm
your father." I sighed and looked v reluctant. And then I
said it was just that the MC and I had been talking about

how different the flat is without him. (This is technically
true. She was banging on about missing Justin—which,
if you ask me, is like missing a migraine—and how
the house didn't feel the same with him gone, and I said
AND SIGMUND TOO and she more or less nodded.)
Sigmund said, "Really?" I said yes. I said the MC seemed
très sad. He looked a bit misty at that, though he said it was
because the tea was too strong.

WEDNESDAY 19 SEPTEMBER

Still no letters! What's wrong with the students in this
school? Are they all on Prozac? Everybody knows that this
is meant to be one of the most **traumatic and stressful** times
of a person's life. You can't open a paper or magazine
without reading some terrifying tale of teenage **suffering and
woe**. The pressure . . . the changes . . . the insecurities . . .
the fear . . . the doubt . . . the raging hormones!!! If you
believe the Sunday supplement, at least half of us are
thinking of hurling ourselves off the nearest bridge!!! But
not at my school. From the OVERWHELMING

LACK OF RESPONSE I've had, you'd think my classmates were all in nursery school with nothing to worry about but lunch. Don't any of them go home and cry? Don't any of them lie awake all night in the dark listening to Led Zeppelin? Don't any of them go home and read the color supplements? They can't all have perfect families. They can't all be happy with their bodies. They can't all be accepted by their peers. It's **ABSOLUTELY** impossible that every alcoholic, addicted, abusive, and sociopathic parent in the country lives **OUTSIDE OF LONDON**!!! I mean, really, what are the odds? Ms. Staples said it's still too early to panic. She said after all, there's a lot going on in the world and even teenagers have more to think about than themselves. As proof that I *do* listen to what people say (even Buskin' Bob!) I pointed out that there's *always* a lot going on in the world. I said aside from the constant warfare and injustice, etc., between 30,000 and 35,000 children died *every day* of preventable causes related to poverty, but it's never stopped anyone from worrying about their hair or whether their hips are too big. I said I didn't really have **A BIT OF TIME**, did I? The first issue comes out in a month!

*　　*　　*

Was so upset that I confided in David (I don't reckon telling him counts anymore than telling the MC since he's a boy and therefore limits his verbal communications to only what is necessary). David said not to worry. If the fiction submissions are anything to go by, I'll be drowning in letters by the end of the week. He said Catriona alone has already submitted SIX poems for the first issue of the magazine, most of which must've been written on her holiday since there's a lot about beaches and sunsets over the rice paddies. He wanted to know where my poem is. I said I was working on it.

As part of my plan to reconcile the parents I had a little chat with the MC tonight. Got her laughing by reminding her of the time Sigmund set fire to the deck chair when he was doing his annual barbecue. She said only Sigmund could burn a deck chair in the rain. I reckoned I heard an affectionate note in her voice, so I told her Sigmund really missed her and said he was hoping they'd get back together someday. She laughed and said well, you never can tell, can you? Let's not forget the Restoration!!! I consider that v hopeful!

THURSDAY 20 SEPTEMBER

Catriona reminded me that the deadline for copy for the
magazine is in two weeks and she hopes I'm planning
to write something. What about my idea about being a
waiter? She really thought that could be v droll. She said
she's often thought of doing a job like that just to see what
it's like. She said that since she intends to be a journalist
she feels that sort of experience would be good to help
her identify with The People. I asked what she meant.
The People **WHO WORK**? Catriona said my sense of
humor is just what the mag needs and that it would be
A CRYING SHAME if I didn't have something in the
very first issue. I explained that I have a lot on my plate at
the moment, and also that I feel there are more important
things in the world than a high-school magazine. I asked
her if she had any idea how many children die *every day* of
poverty-related causes, and she said 33,000, but none of
them were from around here.

After school Marcus helped me make my birthday
invitations on his computer. I brought along a photo of me
when I was just born to work into the design. Marcus said

he always knew I must've been a beautiful baby. I said all babies are beautiful. We put the baby picture at the top and over it we wrote: FROM THIS . . . and under it we wrote: TO THIS . . . And under that we put a photo Marcus took of me this afternoon. Then at the bottom we wrote: COME CELEBRATE SEVENTEEN YEARS OF PROGRESS AT JANET BANDRY'S COSMIC COSTUME BIRTHDAY BASH. Then Marcus did something with the computer and put stars and moons and comets, etc. all over. I think it's **ABSOLUTELY BRILLIANT**! I know my party's not till the end of October, but I don't want to do it all at the **LAST MINUTE** (the way the MC always does). If I give out the invitations now, everyone will have plenty of time to respond and I'll have plenty of time to prepare (and Ethan will have plenty of time to arrange his work schedule!).

Told Sigmund that the MC said she thought there was still a chance they could patch things up. He said really? What about Robert? I said everything passes, everything changes, doesn't it?

FRIDAY 21 SEPTEMBER (Only five weeks and one day till my party!!!)

Everybody was **WOWED** by my invites—even the Hendley. Apparently she **LOVES** dressing up (I love her dressing up too—at least I won't have to look at her face). I told her she should bring her boyfriend. She said what boyfriend would that be? I said I'd heard rumors. She said not about her, I hadn't, but she gave Lila a **V DIRTY LOOK**!!! (Everybody knows what a **BIG MOUTH** Lila has!!!) David couldn't believe I made the invitations myself. I said I had a bit of help from Marcus. David said he should've known. I said why, because the last time David and I worked together on the computer at school I wiped half the magazine from the hard drive? David said that wasn't what he meant at all. Then he said if I want, he'll help me revise for my driving theory test when the time comes. I snapped up the offer. I obviously can't count on any help from *Disha in Love.*

Unlike Catriona Hendley, David really does have amazing organizational skills (possibly due to being the son of a restaurateur) and has arranged for us all to go bowling tonight with Siranee, Sara, and Alice! We haven't seen them since July, so it should be a hoot. Asked Disha if she and Ethan wanted to come since it's his night off, but she said they already had plans. I said can't they be changed? What are you doing, dining with the Queen? Disha laughed. I said just remember you and the Wizard of Oz are coming to my party. She said of course they are . . . unless he has to work. I said he could always come late: I'm expecting it to go on for quite a while!

Sigmund left a present for the MC tonight! It's a book he borrowed from her when they first met. (Sigmund usually gives the MC things like electric toothbrushes, so I reckon this counts as a *Romantic Gesture*—another **FIRST**!) It's not the *same* book, of course (that fell out of his backpack when he was cycling down Marylebone Road in the rain and got run over by a number 18 bus). He wanted her to know he hadn't forgotten about it!!! I showed it to her as soon as she came in with Buskin' Bob. She said it was about time—he borrowed it nearly twenty years ago and she'd never even finished it. But after Buskin' Bob left, I heard her ring Sigmund to thank him and she was so nice and pleasant that at first I thought she was talking to someone else. They went on for approximately twenty-seven minutes, which is something of a record since he moved out (especially since none of it was shouting and screaming!). I definitely consider this another hopeful sign!!!

Still no letters for Aunt K! What am I going to do if she doesn't get any?!! I haven't bothered writing anything else for the mag because I thought solving everybody's problems would be enough to start with. The last thing I need is Catriona pretending to feel sorry for me because I missed out on the **FIRST** issue. David said I could always do an interview if I really have nothing to submit. I said **AN INTERVIEW**? With **WHOM**? It's not like our school is filled with Fascinating Characters or Hollywood Stars. David said how about Mr. Tulliver the caretaker? I said and what would I interview him about? The best way to get old socks out of a toilet? David said Mr. Tulliver used to be in the SAS and has lots of interesting stories about killing people and living on grubs and tree bark, etc. And to think that most journalists want to interview the likes of Spielberg or Madonna—they don't know what they're missing!!!

Have to get ready for bowling. More anon.

SUNDAY 23 SEPTEMBER

It's been **GO! GO! GO!** all weekend. Siranee, Alice, and
Sara all wanted to know where Disha was on Friday night.
I said Disha was in the *Arms of Love*—which seems to
be a lot like being in solitary confinement. Siranee was
v surprised by this news. So was Alice. Alice said Disha's
the last person she'd have expected to behave like that
because she's got a boyfriend—it's something she'd
expect more from **ME**! (Can you believe that?!! I was
too **GOBSMACKED** even to defend myself!!!) Sara,
however, wasn't at all surprised. Sara watches a lot of
daytime telly and says the talk shows are absolutely chock-a-
block with women who totally turn themselves inside out
for men: have their breasts enlarged, dye their hair, become
weightlifters, move to islands off the coast of Africa, etc!!!
And it's not just the unattractive, desperate women either!
Like AIDS, it can happen to *anyone*!!! [Note to self: Ask
Sappho if this could possibly be genetic.] On the brighter
side, the bowling was a hoot and a half! Marcus and David
were good, of course—they have well-developed hand
muscles from playing so many video games—but it was
Siranee who hit so many strikes that the man in the next

lane asked her if she wanted to join his bowling team. After that, everyone came back to mine to watch a film. Ended up getting two videos because we couldn't agree (the males, of course, wanted something violent and not too intellectually taxing, and the females wanted something with character and plot). We couldn't agree on which one to watch first, either, so we played charades instead. The MC and Buskin' Bob came in just as we were starting and wanted to join in. I was still recovering from this shock when I realized that the others were moving around to make room for them! I said pardon me, but fraternizing between my family and my friends is something I tried to discourage (and have done since primary school when the MC first began embarrassing me in public). The Mad Cow and Robert acted like I was making a joke. In the end, it wasn't as bad as I'd feared. There was plenty of hysterical laughter all around. (No one could decide which was funnier—David miming *lap dancer* or Buskin' Bob miming *Bridget Jones's Diary*!!!) Marcus, David, Siranee, Sara, Alice, and I had such a good time that we decided to hang out again last night and watch the videos. Alice said I should ask Disha to come. I said, "You ask her." (Alice did ask her and Disha said she was busy—for a change!)

MONDAY 24 SEPTEMBER

Aunt K finally got two letters today!!! Not that it was exactly worth the wait. I know beggars can't be choosers, but these girls would *never* be selected to go on *Jerry Springer*! Their letters practically redefine **dull and boring**. I swear they could put a starving tiger to sleep. Told David how DISAPPOINTED I am. I said I want exciting problems—abusive uncles, incestuous relationships with brothers and cousins, tortured teens worrying about their sexuality, children driven to the edge by parents who make them scrub the kitchen floor with a toothbrush every morning before school . . . But what do I get? I get *fat thighs* and I *had a fight with my mom*. David said maybe Life is more about imperfect bodies and domestic rows than you'd think from watching telly. [Note to self: If television isn't a reflection of reality, what is it?] At least the letters were easy to answer. (*Half the people in the world have fat thighs—it's not a handicap unless you want to be a catwalk model*, and EVERYBODY *fights with their mother*.) I can only hope the next batch is better!

TUESDAY 25 SEPTEMBER

Discussed the **shallowness and drabness** of most people's lives again with David. He said maybe I should jazz up the letters a bit to make them more exciting. It's tempting, but I don't think it'd work. I mean, the person who wrote the letter will know that it isn't what (s)he said and then Aunt K will lose her credibility. David said anyway, it's still early days yet. Something juicy might be just a letter away. Not today it wasn't.

Sappho and her BUMP (otherwise known as Mount Everest!) came over for supper. Sappho says she isn't sure she and Mags are doing the right thing having a child when the World Situation is so bad. I said things have always been this bad (there are a lot of history programs on the telly, so I know what I'm talking about!) and I didn't see what the problem was. I said it was all right in the past if you were rich or a lord, or something, but everybody else got hanged or shipped to Australia if they so much as nicked a crust of bread. (I found myself thinking that hanging was a better idea so at least their descendants couldn't come back and brainwash your *Best Friend*!) Sappho agreed that life on

141

Earth has never been a picnic for most people, but she said this is the closest we'd ever come to actually destroying the planet. I said well, that's progress, isn't it?

WEDNESDAY 26 SEPTEMBER

As you know, I don't usually hang out with Disha after school anymore because she's always off to meet Ethan before he goes to work, but today he had something else to do, so I went over to hers. Mrs. Paski said it seems like she never sees me anymore. I said that's because she doesn't. D and I hung out in her room. It's amazing how she can get Ethan into conversations that have **ABSOLUTELY NOTHING** to do with him. If we talk about school, she says, "Ethan says when he was in school blah blah blah." If we talk about clothes, she says, "Ethan says that clothes blah blah blah." If we talk about parents, she says, "Ethan says that his parents blah blah blah." Mentioned in passing that it must be possible to get through just one whole sentence without bringing Ethan into it—she used to, didn't she?—and she got all snotty.

142

She wanted to know if I was still cheesed off that he asked her out and not me. I said I was **BORED**, not jealous.

THURSDAY 27 SEPTEMBER

Two more deadly dull letters for Aunt K. The first was from someone who wanted to know if it was true you can't get pregnant the first time (*Answer: No, it isn't true. Aside from the Virgin Mary, who got pregnant* **WITHOUT** *a first time, women have been known to get pregnant without even realizing they had sex!*). The second was from He Loves Me So Much, whose boyfriend is **v possessive and jealous** (*Answer: Jealousy is not a sign of affection; it's a sign of insanity!*). Ms. Staples said I should try to remember that though I think the problems I'm sent are dull and humdrum, to the people writing they're dire and **HUGELY** important. I said it just proves that subjective reality is really unreliable, doesn't it? Then she reminded me that my copy's due in next week. The **SOONER**, the **BETTER**. She said if I was having trouble getting my material together she could always give me a hand. I thanked her, but said that I'm here to **GIVE** help, not take it!

FRIDAY 28 SEPTEMBER

At last! Just when I was beginning to think I was living in a cereal commercial, a **REALLY INTERESTING** letter came for Aunt K today. It's from someone who's worried that her best friend might be seeing one of her teachers!!! Worried Mate's friend told her she met this bloke at the gym she goes to. She said he was one of the trainers and his name was Fred. Worried Mate wanted to get a look at this bloke, of course, so she decided to surprise her friend at the gym one afternoon and get a glimpse. Her friend wasn't there. The person on the desk said her friend hadn't been in for weeks. And **THERE AREN'T ANY TRAINERS NAMED FRED**!!! Worried Mate asked her friend what was going on and her friend told her to **MIND HER OWN BUSINESS**!!! Now she won't talk about Fred **AT ALL**. Worried Mate says they've **NEVER** had any secrets from each other before, so she knows this has to be something really **MAJOR**, like a teacher or a married man. This is the sort of problem that makes an Agony Aunt's day!

Nan came over for supper tonight. It's almost a shame that Buskin' Bob isn't her son; they get on so well. The two of them banged on about the inhumanity of man toward man (and toward every other thing on the planet as far as I can tell) through the whole meal. Apparently Nan's new Jesus group doesn't just sit around reading the Bible all the time; they believe in DOING as much as PRAYING. So Nan's becoming a Christian activist!!! (The Prime Minister worries a lot about hardcore anarchists—just wait till he has to deal with HARDCORE GRANS!!!) Nan said that since she had PERSONAL experience of the **horror** that is war she's even joined a Christian peace group. They believe that the **Thou Shalt Not Kill** commandment should be taken literally—as in you shouldn't kill anyone. She says she reckons that she knows exactly what Jesus would do if He were here now—and it wouldn't be to bomb innocent people who have already suffered enough.

SATURDAY 29 SEPTEMBER

Helped David sort through the fiction submissions for the magazine today because he was a bit overwhelmed (maybe in the rest of Britain the teenagers are all couch potatoes, but at our school at least half of them are writing stories either about *Falling in Love* or saving the world from an alien invasion). To thank me, David took me to lunch at that conveyor-belt sushi restaurant in the West End. It's v high-tech and très trendy. The sushi wasn't bad, but I didn't get much to eat because it's v difficult to hold a conversation and keep up with the dishes drifting past at the same time— it was all right for David because he mainly listens. I told David about Worried Mate's letter. I said if only I had more like that, my first column would be **ABSOLUTE DYNAMITE**. David said it's too bad I can't write to myself, what with all the problems I've had/have in my life. If he hadn't had a mouthful of raw tuna at the time, I think I would've kissed him!!! I told him he was a genius. Why didn't I think of that before? All I have to do is write letters myself. The first one's going to be about how I'm feeling about *Disha in Love*. (She'll never recognize herself—she's much too self-absorbed.) I don't consider this dishonest, because if I wasn't Aunt K I probably would write to her about this situation (God knows, there's nobody else I can talk to about it without sounding **JEALOUS**—which after much soul-searching I absolutely know that I'm not!). I **CAN'T WAIT** to hear what I say!!!

146

SUNDAY 30 SEPTEMBER

Thinking about abandoning both art and literature to pursue a brilliant career in psychotherapy instead. I **DEFINITELY** have a talent for it (must have got more from Sigmund than just small earlobes!). It's taken me **ALL DAY**, but I've written an excruciatingly interesting letter and the reply. Here's what I said to Last Year's Christmas Present (that's **ME!**):

Dear LYCP, First off, you have nothing to apologize for. Of course you're feeling a bit hurt and rejected because your best friend has abandoned you for her new boyfriend. Think of all the hours, days, and years you've spent together. All the Kodak moments and secrets of youth you've shared. It would be strange if you didn't miss her. Especially the way she's carrying on! It's never pleasant to watch someone you respect and admire turn into a zombie right before your eyes. But it's a sad fact of life that many women do change when they get a boyfriend. All of a sudden they're interested in football and how many megabytes their computer has, and they won't wear pink because it reminds **HIM** of some medicine he was given as a child. They stop seeing their old friends not just because they're **OBSESSED** with their New Love, but because they don't want anyone to tell **HIM** that football puts them to sleep and

147

half their wardrobe could belong to Barbie. But what you're feeling
is NOT jealousy. It's SORROW and HURT! What you
have to understand is that, in the words of the poet, nothing lasts
forever—and nothing lasts less time than a passion built only on
physical attraction. In time your friend will come to her senses and
be back to her old self. Before you know it, the two of you will be
sitting around, laughing about what a dork he is!

I feel better already! It's so good that I decided to write a
second letter. This one's from Scared of My Own Shadow.
It's meant to be from someone who has been so affected by
all the things there are to worry about in the world that she's
afraid to go anywhere or do anything. It takes all the strength
she has to go to school. Not only is she afraid of all the things
everybody else is worried about (car accidents, plane crashes,
tornadoes, cholesterol, etc.) but she worries about pianos
falling out of windows and things like that. Aunt K says:

It's a known fact that most accidents happen in the home and are
caused by tea cosies. And it's not just killer tea cosies you have to
worry about either. A man in Putney was watching cricket on
the telly one Saturday afternoon when two men broke into his flat
and shot him in the leg and he bled to death (they were after

someone else). So put on your jacket and get out of the house. Home is the last place you want to be.

MONDAY 1 OCTOBER

Handed in my copy for **ISSUE ONE** to Ms. Staples today, who immediately turned it over to our Editor-in-Chief—who has decided to let Power go to her head! Apparently Catriona (she may write poetry but obviously has the soul of a bureaucrat!) was a bit bothered about the letter from Worried Mate. She reckoned that Old Woolly Jumper, the teachers' unions, and the Minister of Education might be upset about accusing a teacher of professional misconduct. I pointed out to Ms. Staples that no one was accusing anybody of anything. All Worried Mate was saying was that she thinks it might be a teacher because her friend's being **SO** secretive. Also, it's not like this sort of thing doesn't happen all the time, is it? There are precedents! But Ms. Staples said she wasn't certain we should start out with a major controversy. What if we edited the letter a bit to leave out the part about the teacher? I could tell that,

149

besides not wanting to be sued or lose her job or anything like that, Ms. Staples wanted to appease Catriona and not let her feel that she isn't in charge (blessed are the peacemakers, as Nan would say!). I said I wasn't sure that was ethical. And how can my readers be encouraged to write about their real problems if we won't print them? Ms. Staples said I had a point. She said in that case what if Aunt K suggested one or two other reasons why the friend was lying, etc. I said I could live with that.

TUESDAY 2 OCTOBER

Question: HOW BLIND IS A GIRL WHO WILL NOT SEE?

Answer: VERY!!!

Just as I was drifting off to sleep last night I practically fell out of bed when a new thought hit me like an out-of-control juggernaut! Suddenly I **KNEW** why Catriona didn't want to publish Worried Mate's letter. And not because it might upset Old Woolly Jumper either! Because it's **ABOUT HER**!!! I mean, really, how many girls can there be in *one* school who are secretly dating a man they don't want their parents to find out about? (Especially in my school—I read the letters!) Told Disha I've been giving more thought to Catriona's *Secret Love* and it occurred to me that it might be a teacher. Disha said, "Which teacher?" I said I hadn't got as far as thinking about **WHO** it might be; it was just a thought. Disha said if anyone fancied a teacher at our school it would have to be Mr. Plaget, since he's young, single, and attractive. All the other male teachers are either old, married, attractive only if they're being compared to trolls, or all three. That's when another lorry of thought crashed into me and my brain lit up like Piccadilly Circus! I told D about seeing the Hendley and Mr. Plaget leaving school together. Disha said **SO**? Was a student and teacher walking together meant to be **UNUSUAL**? Disha doesn't believe that Mr. Plaget would put his career on the line to date Catriona, esp. with her media connections. Since my own personal experience includes Sigmund putting his marriage on the line to date a woman with twins and a psychotic husband, I find this less impossible than D does. But it is v shocking!!! I've always

151

liked Mr. Plaget. I would've thought he's too smart to fall for someone as obnoxious as the Hendley. But Disha is right about one thing—there is no one else! Must keep a sharp eye out! [Note to self: Why do even intelligent men always fall for the wrong women?]

FRIDAY 5 OCTOBER

The *Roller Coaster of Love* has finally started its descent! (And **NOT A MOMENT TOO SOON**, if you ask me.) Disha and Ethan had a fight!!! She was all quiet and moody at lunch, and then she asked me if I wanted to sleep over. I said I thought she always saw Ethan on Friday nights and that's when she said they're not exactly speaking. I asked her what happened, and she said it was something that wasn't worth discussing. As soon as we got to her room she lit up a cigarette. I reminded her that she doesn't smoke anymore. She said she didn't *usually* but she was feeling a bit stressed. I said I didn't see how getting lung cancer was going to make her feel less stressed. I said, "So are you going to tell me what's wrong?" and she said,

"NOTHING." Then she started to cry. I said she ought to be angry, not miserable. She wanted to know how I could say that when I didn't even know what had happened. (Well, I WOULD know if someone would tell me!) I said because she isn't the sort of person to argue over something stupid like how to boil water. (Sigmund and the MC have had several fights about that one!) So it must be something Ethan did. She said it wasn't really anything he did—it was more that they have different views of things. I said well, of course they do. He's a boy and she's a girl—what did she expect?

SATURDAY 6 OCTOBER

Got home to find the MC scrubbing around the bathroom taps with a toothbrush. I asked if this was some sort of post-menopausal symptom or if the Queen was coming around. She said Marcella made an unkind remark about her housekeeping standards last time and she didn't want it repeated. I said you mean the Hotspurettes are coming HERE? AGAIN? She said she'd told me. Wanted to go back to Disha's but the Mad Cow mooed and **PUT HER HOOF DOWN** (right on **ME**, as per usual!). I tried to explain that Disha's in a state of emotional turmoil brought on by love and needs me. The MC said that Disha can look forward to many unhappy years of emotional turmoil brought on by love, so I'll have plenty more opportunities to be supportive—today it's *her* turn. She said she'd told them I'd take them to Camden Market. Apparently they'd like that. (Please note that she didn't tell **ME** I was taking them to the market and obviously doesn't care that I won't like it. And I thought it was the stepchildren who were meant to be treated like second-class citizens!) Immediately rang Disha and got her to come along. She said at least it would take her mind off her aching, breaking heart. Which wasn't true, of course. If you ask me, there's nothing short of a nuclear war that could take Disha's mind off her bleedin' heart. She was in **ABSOLUTE Zombie Girl** mode all afternoon. She wasn't crying (miraculously!), but she looked like that was only because she had no tears left. She clutched her mobe the whole time we were out, just in case Ethan rang to apologize (but for **WHAT**?!!). And she didn't really speak (unless you count the occasional grunt and nod—which I don't). Being terminally **SELF-ABSORBED** themselves, the Deadly

154

Duo didn't notice Disha's state. Marcella kept up a running commentary on everything we saw (the child's like walking background music!), and Lucrezia held up her end by throwing a **MAJOR** hissy fit because she wanted to buy a blue top like the one Marcella bought in green, only they didn't have it in blue. Walked off and left her to it but she came straight after us, screaming that **EVERYONE ELSE** gets what they want! (How can this child possibly be related to Buskin' Bob?) I said that actually it isn't true that everyone else gets what they want. I said that **MOST OF THE PEOPLE** in the world don't even get what they really need—never mind what they want. She said I sounded just like her father and kicked me! Through all this Disha was constantly testing her phone to make sure it was working and said nothing. Only when we were leaving the market did D say it seemed to her that Lucrezia has some behavioral problems. I said she couldn't imagine how grateful I was to have her point that out to me. Disha went home (presumably to cry, or at least moan in anguish, in the privacy of her room), and the Deadly Duo and I went to get a video. Lucrezia got to pick because she screams loudest. (Marcella says there's no point arguing with Lucrezia because even if you win she'll ruin it for you. I asked if she doesn't find her sister **EXHAUSTING** and she said yes. I felt really sorry for Marcella even though she never stops talking. I know how much I suffer from being the sister of Justin Bandry—but on the list of Most Irksome Siblings in the Universe he's **WAY** below Lucrezia Hotspur. He's like a goldfish next to her shark!) Marcella and I played backgammon after supper while Lucrezia watched her film and Buskin' Bob and the MC sat in the kitchen drinking wine and singing "Big Yellow Taxi" and "He's Only a Hobo" over and over. (I'm surprised the neighbors don't call the cops—I was v tempted to call them myself.) I learned a lot about Marcella's mother the actress and her stepfather the entrepreneur. Apparently they're v busy **ALL THE TIME** (being on telly and making money). That's why the Deadly Duo go to boarding school in the week. Marcella said that although Buskin' Bob is a pain in the bum about what you can eat, etc., at least he hangs out with them. I said what about the guitar? Marcella said she's learned to live with it. If you ask me, it's like learning to live underwater.

TUESDAY 9 OCTOBER

Catriona was banging on about her costume for my party today. She's coming as a belly dancer—even though she doesn't actually have a belly. (It's a good thing I didn't decide to have a Middle Eastern theme for my party or *all* the really slim girls would've come as belly dancers and I would've wound up being an aubergine!) Anyway, the Hendley's monologue reminded me that I haven't done anything about my own costume yet! I'm going as Trinity from *The Matrix* (thanks to the Dark Phase, **BLACK** is something I can do!). Disha doesn't know what she's going to be yet. I said it is only a little over **TWO WEEKS** away you know. She said that was plenty of time. I said only if you're planning to come as a twenty-first-century teenager. Marcus and David are being *v secretive* about their costumes. They both want theirs to be a surprise.

WEDNESDAY 10 OCTOBER

Woke up in the middle of the night with **THE MOST AWFUL** thought in my head. What if the MC invites Buskin' Bob to my party? Even worse—what if he decides he's the entertainment? (One chorus of "Where Have All the Flowers Gone?" and my social life wouldn't be toast, it'd be the crumbs at the bottom of the toaster. I could never live it down!) Had a word with the MC over the organic muesli this morning. She gets all huffy if you say anything even the teensiest bit critical of Buskin' Bob, so all I said (très casually) was, was she planning to see him next weekend? She said he's taking the Deadly Duo camping and since she has no intention of leaving the party without a chaperone she's not going with them. (Apparently she made that mistake when Justin was my age and came home to find the police on the doorstep. I think she's making it up. I have **NO** memory of this **AT ALL**! You can see what I have to deal with here, can't you?) Then she wanted to know why I wanted to know. I said no reason.

THURSDAY 11 OCTOBER

The *Roller Coaster of Love* has peaked again. Apparently Disha and the Wizard of Oz have made up (oh, JOY!!!). She was all bubbly and happy and talking again today. Of course, since she only seems to have one topic of conversation when she isn't depressed into silence, it was all about Ethan. Blah blah blah . . . I think I liked it better when they'd fallen out.

A few more letters are trickling in to Aunt K but none of them are any more riveting than the first lot. *Dear Aunt K, My parents won't let me have a nose job . . . (Answer: Save the plastic surgery for when you're over forty and really need it.) Dear Aunt K, There's a boy I like who seems to like me but he hasn't asked me out, so I'm not really sure how he feels. What should I do? (Answer: Ask him out. You'll know from his reaction exactly how he feels.) Dear Aunt K, I've tried every diet there is but I'm still a size fourteen. Should I have my lips sewn together? (Answer: I can tell you from personal experience that dieting makes you fat, so the first thing you should do is stop doing that. And if you sew your lips closed and get a cold, you'll die because you can't breathe. Being a size fourteen is a lot better than being dead.)* Both David and Ms. Staples say not to worry about the meager (in every sense of the word!) letters, as once the first issue hits the stands I'll be deluged. I said I hoped so. At the moment I'm being dampened to death.

FRIDAY 12 OCTOBER

I swear to God Nan spends more time at ours now that her son's in Kilburn than she did when he lived here! She rolled up tonight with a sign that says THERE IS NO SUCH THING AS A GOOD WAR and her overnight bag. Turns out she's spending the night at ours because she's going on some demo tomorrow. I said wasn't she going to feel a bit out of place among all the squatters, hardcore anarchists, and travelers who usually show up for these things? Nan said why should she? I said because she's **OLD**. Nan said even old people have a right to their opinion. That's what democracy is all about. I said I didn't really see the point in taking to the streets, then. The government was elected to do its job and that's what it's doing. I said that's what democracy is all about too!!! Nan says it can't do the job **SHE** elected it to do if it doesn't know what she thinks.

SATURDAY 13 OCTOBER

Even though I haven't exactly got back into the Dark Phase, I'm happy to be able to say that my personal growth and development continue at a rapid pace. Had a completely **NEW** experience today (and for once it wasn't all bad!). Without consulting **ME**, the MC decided that we should **ALL** go on the demo with Nan. I said I had a lot of homework and really couldn't waste time being arrested. The MC said she didn't see any problem since I never do it till Sunday night anyway and we'd be released by then. She said wasn't I meant to be a writer for the school magazine? She reckoned an article on an antiwar protest would be more interesting than writing about what the cafeteria was serving for lunch. I had to admit that she had a point. Especially if I **DID** get arrested. And since Disha and the Wizard are back together, I wasn't going to be hanging out with her. Rang Marcus to see if he wanted to come (he did). Then rang David to see if he wanted to come too. David wanted to know if I'd already asked Marcus. Then he said he'd wait for the next demo. I asked how he knew there'd be one? He said because this one wasn't going to do any good. I haven't seen so many policemen in one place since I watched that documentary on the Miners' Strike. (God knows where they all are when you really want one—there certainly weren't any about the time Mr. Burl's scooter was nicked!) I was **ASTONISHED** at how many old people were there (and some of them were even older than Nan!). I was expecting riot police with shields and horses and clubs, etc. like they put on for May Day, but it was all pretty civilized. No incidents of violence—unless you count the balloon filled with tomato sauce Nan threw at a police van (she missed). Nan was cautioned by a copper who was shocked that a woman who had been through the war would behave like that. Nan said she was behaving like that *because* she'd been through the war. Marcus thanked me for asking him along. He thinks the MC, Buskin' Bob, and Nan are all brilliant (another first!). He said he wished his family would show more interest in politics instead of just watching telly and destroying the house with DIY projects.

SUNDAY 14 OCTOBER

Had a brainwave (I really should do the Mensa test—
I have to be at least **NEAR** genius!). I don't reckon the
parents are ever going to patch things up if they're never
together, and they're never together because either she's
out or Robert's sitting in the kitchen strumming his guitar.
But next weekend Robert will be in a tent somewhere with
the Deadly Duo, so I rang Sigmund and invited him to the
party. He was **THRILLED**. He kept saying, "You really
want me to be there?" I said of course I did: the MC
would need some company.

MONDAY 15 OCTOBER

Since Disha was **OTHERWISE ENGAGED**, got
Marcus to come to the goth shoe shops of Camden with
me to look for just the right combination of leather and
metal. Marcus said he hoped I appreciated that this is
something he would only do for **ME**, since boot
shopping is just below torture on the list of activities he

tries to avoid. He was pretty good for the first hour, but by the time we hit the third shop he was starting to grumble. He said he didn't know why I had to try on every pair of boots I saw—especially since they were all basically the same. I explained that they were only the same to the untrained eye. Finally found the **PERFECT** pair (in the last shop, of course!). They're v futuristic. Marcus couldn't believe how much they cost. He thought I was mad to spend that much on a pair of boots I'm never going to wear again. I said that was the beauty of it. Since I'm not wearing them out in the street, I can return them after the party and get my money back. Marcus says he admires my mind even though it scares him a bit.

TUESDAY 16 OCTOBER

David wanted to know why I didn't ask HIM to go shopping with me. I said because he hates shopping. He said so does Marcus. Also, *The Matrix* is one of his all-time favorite films, which qualifies him to choose the right boots. Marcus is a Jackie Chan fan, which *obviously* disqualifies him. I said if he wants, he can come with me after school next Friday to get in the supplies for the party. He said he wants.

WEDNESDAY 17 OCTOBER

Mr. Belakis managed to wheedle some of the lottery loot out of Old Woolly Jumper so the A-level art classes can have a real exhibition in the spring and invite guests besides our parents. I saw that artist Tracey Emin on telly once and apparently she got a load of money for her bed—which, if you ask me, just looked like it hadn't been made in a while. I reckoned I could get even more for my bed and really **SHAKE UP** the Art World (not only hasn't my bed been made in a while but the headboard's been set on fire at least three times—and it has the name of every boy I fancied in primary school scratched into it). But Mr. Belakis says he prefers Inspiration to Installation. He's given us all a project to form the focus for the exhibition, which is something about our families. Marcus is doing a ginormous canvas depicting the history of his family from their beginnings in Africa to winding up in England. My family's history isn't nearly as interesting as Marcus's (no slave trade, no Jamaican rebels, no poor immigrants with all their possessions in a cardboard box and a picture of the Queen), so I'm doing a family portrait. I was going to do just my immediate family (the Mad Cow, Sigmund, me, and possibly Geek Boy—if I can find a photo of him where he doesn't look like a throwback to our primal past), but Mr. Belakis said that including my un-immediate family would be a good challenge for someone of my talent and potential. Think I'll do Sappho now, since pregnant is easier to do than an infant.

THURSDAY 18 OCTOBER

All I can say is, we **DEFINITELY** live in stressful times! (It's a wonder the whole planet isn't on drugs, if you ask me!) Marcus and I stayed after school again to work on our art projects. Mr. Belakis rushed off afterward, but before Marcus and I left to get the bus, I went to the ladies' while

he took the art-room key to Mr. Tulliver. (I didn't really
have to go, but I knew that by the time I got home—
public transport being what it is—I'd be desperate!) I was
repairing the damage the ravages of the afternoon had done
to my face—Marcus and I had been laughing so much that
my eyes had run—when I knocked my mascara off the
counter and it rolled under the sink. I bent down to pick
it up and GASPED OUT LOUD!!! Right in front
of my eyes, stuffed behind one of the pipes, was a
SUSPICIOUS PACKAGE! (You really never think
it's going to happen to YOU, do you?) It was small
and in a brown bag. I didn't panic, of course, but I was
CAUTIOUS (there's been a lot on the telly about just
this sort of thing!). I put all my makeup back in my case
and raced out to get Marcus. Marcus, of course, is an artist
not a fighter, but he didn't hesitate for a nanosecond—he
went straight in! (It was a side of him I'd never seen before
and I was v impressed!) Marcus thought it was too small
to be a bomb. I said if you can put a bomb in the heel of
a SHOE (which apparently you can), the package could
probably hold TWO bombs. Marcus was all for removing
it and seeing what it was (is that FEARLESS or what?),
but I reminded him that that's EXACTLY what you're

not meant to do. The office was shut by then, but the news is always on at ours (so Buskin' Bob can keep up with the injustices each new day brings), so I knew exactly what to do. I rang 999 on my mobe. I said I had reason to believe that there was an explosive device in the ladies' of the main building at the Bere Road Secondary School. The police said to wait outside and they'd be **RIGHT WITH US**. All I can say is, I don't know how the police reckon time but it's not the way the rest of us do. **HOURS PASSED**. Marcus kept looking at his watch and telling me how many more minutes had passed. Five . . . ten . . . twelve-and-a-half . . . fourteen . . . twenty . . . I was just about to ring the coppers back when Mr. Tulliver rolled up. He wanted to know what we were doing, standing there like we were waiting for a bus. I told him about the suspicious package. Mr. Tulliver is fat and bald and doesn't look like he was ever in the SAS (unless it was as a cook), but like Marcus he didn't hesitate. He said this was just the sort of thing he'd been trained for and vanished inside. When another **EON** had passed, Marcus decided to go after him. I said I was certain we would've heard the bomb go off if Mr. Tulliver's training had let him down, but Marcus said maybe it wasn't an explosive; maybe it just leaked a lethal gas and poor Mr.

Tulliver was passed out on the floor of the ladies'. I said we weren't in an episode of *Batman* but Marcus wouldn't listen. He didn't come back either. By the time the police finally turned up (no lights or siren—you can only wonder what they consider an emergency!), I was feeling V ANXIOUS but I remained calm and explained about the suspicious package and the two brave men who had gone to investigate (and who, for all I knew, were BOTH passed out on the floor of the ladies'!). The first cop wanted to know why I thought it was a bomb. I said well, what else would I think it was, stuffed behind the sink like that? The second cop wanted to know if the rest of us could hear laughing. I'd never heard Mr. Tulliver's laugh before. (Well, I wouldn't, would I? He's usually fixing something or fishing something out of the biology pond in a professional manner.) But I recognized Marcus's. I said maybe it wasn't laughter; maybe it was hysteria. It was laughter. Mr. Tulliver and Marcus came striding toward us. Mr. Tulliver was holding up the paper bag and both of them were laughing so much there were tears in their eyes. Marcus said I should've seen Mr. Tulliver in SAS mode. It was so much like a film that Marcus hadn't even been frightened, he'd just stood by the door watching him sneak up on the bomb—ready to run. Only it wasn't a bomb . . . it was a packet of cigarettes. The coppers said that if they had a quid for every bomb scare they'd investigated in the last few weeks, they could take early retirement. Marcus wanted to know how many bombs they *had* found, and the coppers said that so far the cigarettes were the only things they'd discovered that would actually light.

FRIDAY 19 OCTOBER

Marcus thinks I should include the Hotspurs in my family portrait. I said that though it's true you can't get much more un-immediate than Buskin' Bob, Marcella, and Lucrezia, I have my doubts about them still being in the family by the time of the exhibition. Marcus wanted to know what made me say that. He thought they all seemed pretty well embedded in the family. I said he shouldn't always go by appearances.

SUNDAY 21 OCTOBER

Spent the **WHOLE** day sorting out my costume for the party. I'm going to look so cool, people who come near me are going to need a jumper! Got a cheap black wig in the market as I'm not risking dyeing my hair after what happened last time.

MONDAY 22 OCTOBER

The first issue of *Speak Out!* hit the stands today!!! It looks **FANTASTIC**!!! Ms. Staples said we should all be proud of ourselves (something you **DON'T** have to tell Catriona Hendley twice!). It was sold out by lunchtime. I heard quite a few people talking about **MY** column! Everybody thinks the teacher in Worried Mate's letter must be Mr. Plaget. They all want to know who Aunt K is, of course. Even Disha was nagging me. A few short months ago I might have weakened and told her, since I've never had any secrets from D, but now that she's keeping me at a distance, I found it easy to lie. I said I had **NO IDEA**.

I said it was something Ms. Staples cooked up and **NO ONE** on the magazine knows who it is but her. Then, very casual like, I asked her what she thought of the letter from Last Year's Christmas Present. She said she hadn't read it. She said she'd read the one from He Loves Me So Much and didn't think much of the advice, so she'd stopped after that. She said it didn't seem to her that Aunt K knew v much about *Love*. I said that didn't mean she didn't know a lot about insanity.

Gave D her birthday present at lunch since she was meeting Ethan straight after school for their **PRIVATE** celebration. Got her that top we saw in Gap. I said I knew she couldn't wear it now, but, judging by what you read in magazines, there's a good chance she'll have another boyfriend in her lifetime and he might like orange.

172

TUESDAY 23 OCTOBER

I could hardly believe it but when I checked the mailbox
this afternoon there were four letters for Aunt K! (This
represents a definite deluge!) Ms. Staples said hadn't she
told me this would happen? I said I'd never really doubted
her but *she* knew better than anyone that the *Creative
Spirit* is v sensitive and easily demoralized. (Great artists
and writers are known for self-mutilation, suicide, and
drinking themselves to death—and what is that but the cry
for help of a *Delicate Soul*?) Ms. Staples said she never
really thought of writing an agony column as requiring
a great amount of *Creativity* (so even *she* has her
limitations!). I said I didn't really see much difference
between writing a story, a poem, or a letter to Spotty
and Desperate. Not that these new letters are any more
interesting than the others, of course. I really do
understand that to a person with dandruff or wobbly
thighs there isn't anything much worse that could happen,
but reading all these letters has made me realize anew how
shallow and trivial the lives of most people are. (And
I thought it was just MY family!) Ms. Staples said my
column has certainly generated a lot of interest. I said good

173

advice is much more relevant to people's lives than poems about dusk in Indonesia, isn't it? She said not only among the student body. Apparently Old Woolly Jumper wants a word with her.

WEDNESDAY 24 OCTOBER

As you know, I have nothing but respect and admiration for Ms. Staples, so you can imagine how **SHOCKED** I was today to discover that she's a snitch! She told Mr. Cardogan who Aunt K is! She said she had no choice. So the upshot was that I had to go and see him!!! Old Woolly Jumper and I are not unacquainted, of course, but our meetings have always been about things like lateness and talking at the same time as a teacher. Mr. Cardogan started out by telling me how brilliant the magazine is and how proud he is of all of us. Then he went on to praise my column for being so practical and down-to-earth. He said he was pleasantly surprised. I said, "Really?" He said he'd always thought I had a rather flamboyant imagination. I said having a *Passionate Heart and Soul* didn't mean you don't know how to change a fuse. He said he also liked my sense of humor. I was just starting to think that I'd been worried over nothing when Old Woolly Jumper let me have it. He wanted to know if I was aware that there were rumors **FLYING ALL OVER THE PLACE** since my column came out. I said a school is like a village—there are always rumors flying about. He said not about one of his teachers going out with a student, there aren't. I said if he'd read my column, he'd know that Aunt K pooh-poohed the whole teacher idea and suggested that the mysterious boyfriend might be something much worse, like a traveler or a Womble. He said he accepted that I wasn't personally responsible for the gossip but he would appreciate it in future if I stuck to things like diets and skin care. I said would Life? Would Life content itself with the odd spot and the need for garlic? I said I didn't think so. He said he'd like us both to try. I said I'd see what I could do, of course. But I have **ABSOLUTELY** no intention of letting Aunt K be threatened or bullied by the reactionary forces of the Establishment. Freedom of the press is at stake!!! Disha wanted to know what Old Woolly Jumper wanted. I said he was wondering if I would like to do an interview with him for the magazine.

*   *   *

On a more positive note, Aunt K had **FIVE** more letters today! One Fat Bum, one Small Breasts, one My Boyfriend Would Rather Hang Out with His Mates Than with Me, one The Only Films My Boyfriend Wants to See Are Thrillers, and one My Boyfriend Says I Talk Too Much (*Answers: Learn to live with it and Dump him*). It made me think once again about how très **IRONIC** life is. I mean, I've worked really hard for years (or at least months!) trying to write fiction with little success (though Ms. Staples did have a lot of good things to say about the story I wrote in the spring)— and now here I am excelling at **NONFICTION**. What if it is genetic? What if I've inherited psychoanalytical skills from Sigmund (even though he doesn't really have that many) when my *Heart and Soul* cries out to be a novelist—or maybe an artist or poet? Am I to be **thwarted and frustrated** because of a mere accident of birth?

There **MUST** be a blue moon tonight! Got Disha to come with me, David, and Marcus after school to the new très trendy café by the canal as a late birthday treat for her. (Apparently Ethan's working.) You can sit outdoors (**YES**—even in **ENGLAND**!!!) all year long because

176

they've got heaters and umbrellas. Marcus said you have to hand it to British ingenuity and David said he reckoned it was more likely to be American technology because Americans like to improve **EVERYTHING** but the British have always just muddled through and made do. We were mucking about, having a few laughs, when I thought I saw Ethan walk past. I said, "Hey, there's Ethan!" David and Marcus both swung around like turnstiles, but Disha said it wasn't him. I said I was sure it was and she should go after him and bring him over, but she was **ADAMANT**. She said she thought she'd be able to pick her own boyfriend out of a crowd. Marcus said he was beginning to doubt that this bloke actually exists. David said maybe he's the Invisible Australian. Disha said she had to go.

THURSDAY 25 OCTOBER

It's a sad and galling fact of my life that ever since I was little, the small, dull minds of my relatives have constantly accused me of having **TOO MUCH IMAGINATION** (as if there is such a thing, right?). Even Disha Paski (you remember her—she used to be my best friend in the universe) has been known to suggest that sometimes I get carried away. Well, they can scoff **ALL THEY WANT**— guess what I saw today? Something that will force the doubters to think again about my instincts and judgment, that's what!!! David and I went to the high street after school to get me a driving handbook. We were walking back to mine when I saw Mr. Plaget's Beetle stopped at a light (you can't miss it—most of it's orange!). I was just about to wave when I realized who was sitting beside him! Oh, yes! It was none other than Catriona of-course-I-don't-have-a-boyfriend Hendley!!! She was smiling and shaking her hair about the way she does. I pulled David into a doorway so they wouldn't see us. He wanted to know what was wrong with me. I said I'd just seen Catriona in Mr. Plaget's car. David said, "**AND**?" and I said I had reason to believe that Catriona was the girl in Worried Mate's letter. David said, "And why is that?" I said, "Call it a hunch." He said he'd rather call it a wild guess and that it was bad enough that people are whispering about poor Mr. Plaget without me joining in. He is **ABSOLUTELY CERTAIN** that Mr. Plaget is not going out with Catriona or any other student. I said maybe, but you don't have to

178

be Einstein to work out that two and two makes four, do you? David said actually Einstein flunked maths, so he probably wouldn't've worked it out. David said the fact is that Catriona's in Mr. Plaget's advanced calculus class and it's not a big deal if he gives her a lift. I said I still thought it was v suspicious. David wanted to know if I remembered when I thought *he* was interested in Catriona? I said *oh, that*.

The driving manual is nearly **FOUR HUNDRED PAGES LONG**!!! I really think that's a bit harsh. I mean, how can anyone be expected to remember **EVERYTHING** that's in it? (Especially someone who's doing her A-levels!! There is only so much space in the human brain, after all!) You'd have to have a photocopier memory.

Love's Roller Coaster has done another deep dive. Disha rang in tears again tonight. (She'll dehydrate if she doesn't watch out!) She had yet another fight with Ethan. I asked what it was about this time. She said, "**NOTHING**" (between sobs!!!). Which, of course, is what she always says. I said I really didn't think this was the way a relationship was meant to be. Not unless you'd been married for a while.

119

I said was she sure she was in *Love* and not just having a **nervous breakdown**? Disha said nothing that was really worth having was ever easy. I said a lot of things that weren't worth having (like AIDS) weren't easy either. Disha said that's what she loves about me, I always make her laugh. I said it didn't sound to me like she was laughing—unless it was through her tears. I said why won't she TELL ME what's going on? She said it's really no big deal. Also, I wouldn't understand (she obviously doesn't know WHO she's talking to!!!). And she already knows what I'd say. I said I don't see how *she* could know when I don't.

FRIDAY 26 OCTOBER

Marcus has finally paid his father back for the parking ticket, so he took me shopping for party supplies in the car this afternoon. It's so long since I've been in a real supermarket that the lighting, etc. practically made me SWOON! It was weird to be totally engulfed in food and not actually be able to smell any of it. Marcus said he never noticed. I started reading the labels on everything (it's

ASTOUNDING how even someone with a strong
character like mine can be influenced without even
realizing it!). Marcus wanted to know what I was doing.
I said I was just checking for sugar and GM soya, etc.
Marcus said I was mad. He said even crisps have sugar in
them and if I kept that up we wouldn't have
ANYTHING to eat. Dropping Buskin' Bob's standards,
we filled a whole trolley with unsuitable soft drinks and
snacks!!! Then we went to the party shop and got balloons
(black and purple) and streamers (also black and purple).
And then we went to the cheap place across from the tube
to get prizes. The MC noticed the carrier bags right off.
She immediately started going on about how I was
destroying the market stalls and small grocers of London.
I said, "It's my party and I'll buy where I want to."
Marcus thought that was HILARIOUS but the Mad Cow
didn't even crack a smile. Marcus said he'd come round
tomorrow to help me blow up the balloons, etc. I decided
not to mention that David is coming too in case he gets
in one of his moods. (I don't know why it's women who
have a reputation for being temperamental—I find blokes
v touchy!)

*   *   *

181

Told Disha about seeing Catriona with Mr. Plaget. Disha thinks I should dedicate my brain to science. She said it'd distract them from human cloning for centuries trying to work it out. I said David saw them too (which he would've if he'd been looking). I said they seemed to be having a good time. D said he was probably just giving her a lift, which isn't a crime in this country yet. I said a lift to *where*? Disha said a lift *home*.

Sometimes it almost surprises even me how I'm always right (though I do realize, of course, that I'm lucky to be so intuitive!). This afternoon Disha discovered that Lila and the Hendley have had a **MAJOR FALLING-OUT**!!!! I'm willing to concede that Mr. Plaget *might* just have happened to give Catriona a lift home because she broke her foot leaving the school grounds or something, but not when at the **VERY SAME TIME** Catriona and Lila have stopped speaking. I mean, really—how can that be a coincidence? Catriona must've worked out who Worried Mate is. Disha said that wasn't what Lila told *her*. Lila said it was over something Lila borrowed that she can't find to give back. Pull the other one, that's what I say. David, of course, agreed with Disha. He asked if it had ever occurred to me that the letter might not be about Catriona? I said no.

SATURDAY 27 OCTOBER

It's been **GO**! **GO**! **GO**! all day, but I have to **STOP** for just a few minutes to tell you what happened now because I'm **V UPSET**!!! (Now I know how that woman who found a tarantula in her bunch of bananas must've felt! Surprise doesn't even **BEGIN** to cover it!) David, Marcus, and I were putting up fairy lights in the living room (Marcus's idea—so they'll look like stars!) when the phone rang. It was Disha. She said she was **REALLY, REALLY** sorry but she's not going to be able to come tonight because she's got the worst period pains any woman has ever had since time began. I couldn't believe she was using the old cramps excuse on **ME OF ALL PEOPLE**!!! I practically invented it! I said why didn't she just take a painkiller? She said she's been eating them like sweets but they don't help.

I said what about a hot-water bottle? She said that didn't work either. I said what about Ethan? Wasn't he looking forward to meeting everyone? She said had I forgotten that they'd had a fight? And anyway, he has to work. I said so why can't she come on her own? She said because she's got the worse period pains any woman has ever had since time began. I was TOO hurt and angry to argue. I said well, thanks for the birthday surprise and slammed down the phone! Then I burst into tears. David and Marcus were v comforting. David said maybe Disha really is in pain (she would be if she'd told me to my face!). I said yeah and maybe there's a flock of pigs flying over London. I said I knew she was lying. David said not to let this ruin the party for me. He gave me a hug. Marcus said you've still got US. He gave me a hug too. I put on a brave face and said of course I wouldn't let the petty insanity of Disha Paski destroy my big day. But I was lying. How can I enjoy myself when my *Best Friend* has dumped me ON MY BIRTHDAY?!! I know, of course, that you can't rely on anyone in this world, but I never dreamed that included Disha! I'll get dressed and put a smile on my face, but I'll be crying on the inside. (The dark, bitter tears of wisdom!)

SUNDAY 28 OCTOBER

The party was an **INCREDIBLE, GINORMOUS** success!!! *Everybody* said so. The decorations were brilliant, the costumes were brilliant, and there was a lot of food. Even Catriona Hendley was v enthusiastic! (Which could be because she won the prize for Best Costume, as two of the judges were men—even though one's an **EXPERT** on human behavior and the other has his mind on **HIGHER THINGS**. I reckon this is evidence in favor of the Nature over Nurture argument!) Anyway, guess who David came as? **NEO FROM THE MATRIX**! I was **COMPLETELY SURPRISED**. But I was even more surprised when I saw Marcus. He came as the bloke from *The Matrix* too! (And if you think I was **STUNNED**, you should've seen their faces when they saw each other!) Of course, this being Life on Planet Earth, it wasn't all gaiety and laughter—there were a few tense moments. The first was when I went into the kitchen to show the MC my costume and discovered the three Hotspurs drinking tea (they all looked like they'd been through the wash!). I said I thought they were going camping. The MC said maybe I hadn't noticed but it'd been pissing down since last night.

Their tent collapsed and they had to come home. (Since I didn't want to start a fight right then, I didn't point out that this ISN'T their home!) This was followed by some high drama because, even though it was agreed that the Deadly Duo would watch telly in Justin's room and not bother me and my guests, Lucrezia went BERSERK because she wanted to come to the party. So we didn't all end up with migraines, I said she and Marcella could come for ten minutes. Then she went even more berserk because she wanted to wear a costume. This time it was the MC who caved in like a sandcastle and said she'd see what she could find. (Lucrezia came as a lampshade!) The next tense moment was when Sigmund turned up with a bottle of champagne. Sigmund was as surprised to see Buskin' Bob and his progeny as everybody else was to see him! Using the skills he's developed over decades of professional psychoanalysis, Sigmund asked the MC why she was looking at him like that. She said because she hadn't known that he was coming. (BOTH of them then glared at ME, of course! I sometimes think the only reason they had me was so they'd have someone to blame for every little thing that goes wrong.) I said it is my SEVENTEENTH BIRTHDAY, you know, and, unless the Mad Cow had

186

some **dark secret** to reveal, Sigmund is my father. Sigmund started muttering that he didn't want to be in the way (something that has never bothered him before), but Buskin' Bob (obviously très affected by being in a collapsing tent in a monsoon with Lucrezia) made the first joke I've ever heard him make (possibly the ONLY joke he's ever made!). Robert said he wasn't going to let a man with a bottle of champagne leave. Not after the weekend he was having. Sigmund sat right down. He loves to hear other people's problems even when he isn't being paid by the hour. [Note to self: Is this because it's his job or because it makes him feel better about the mess he's made of his own life?]

Rang Disha first thing this morning to tell her what a BRILLIANT time we all had. (I know this may sound a wee bit petty, but I asked Aunt K and she said it would be wrong not to, since true friendship is based on honesty.) Disha said she'd thought I was angry with her. I said I was a bit irked but I got over it. Anyway, I was more HURT than angry. I said I just don't understand why she's being so weird. She said she's not being weird; I just don't understand how hard it is being in *Love*. I said I hadn't realized it was meant to be *hard*—I thought it was meant

to be fun. If she's anything to go by, I don't really want
to find out what it's like. Disha said the party sounded
really excellent. She was sorry she missed it. She said she
supposed everybody wondered where she was, and I said
no, they were getting used to her not being around.

Sigmund gave me my first driving lesson today! (We hadn't
gone around the block when he wanted to know what the
rattling sound was—he thought the exhaust was falling
off again. I said not to worry, it was just the bottles for
recycling in the boot.) All things considered, I thought it
went v well. I feel I have a natural talent for driving as well
as for literature, art, and problem solving. Sigmund took
me to a deserted car park on an industrial estate behind
King's Cross where I could drive around without having
to worry about anybody hitting us (London drivers are
NOTORIOUSLY bad). There's more to this driving lark
than you'd think, though, especially if your parents are old
fogeys who still drive a manual! It's just as well there were
no other cars about as it was all très intense. Nonetheless,
I've already mastered starting and stopping. (I'm particularly
good at stopping because changing gear is v tricky and you
have to do things with your feet and your hands all at

the same time.) I did suggest that maybe it was time the
Bandrys joined the age of technology and got an automatic,
and Sigmund said he'd sooner get a new daughter than a
new car. (Whoever said psychoanalysts don't have a sense
of humor? The man's practically a laugh a line!) While we
were waiting for the Mini to recover from having its engine
flooded (apparently MY fault!), Sigmund said he'd had
a good time at my party (all things considered!). I said,
"You mean all things like Buskin' Bob considered?" He said
more like the fact that no one had known he was coming.
Sigmund said Robert seemed like a nice bloke. I said you're
just saying that because you think your professional
reputation would be damaged if it got out that you'd like to
feed Robert's liver to the wild dogs of Clapham. Sigmund
said no, he really likes Robert. He thinks he has some v
sound ideas. I said and which one would that be? I said
he'd feel differently if Buskin' Bob had had his guitar with
him. Sigmund said it looked to him like the MC was v keen
on Robert. He certainly didn't get the impression she was
thinking of dumping him and getting back with the father
of her children any time this millennium. I said you can
never tell with women, though, can you? They're enigmas.
He said, "Speak for yourself!"

189

Invited Disha around tonight but she's too depressed to enjoy herself. She said she's never felt like this before. Can't eat . . . can't sleep . . . thinks about him all the time . . . I said it sounded to me like she's ill. She said only with *Love*. If you ask me, *Love* should come with a **Government Health Warning**.

MONDAY 29 OCTOBER

Since it's half-term, this was day two of my driving lessons. I only stalled four (possibly five) times AND I got into THIRD GEAR! Got a little confused with the lights and the indicators and couldn't find the horn, but all in all I made quite a bit of progress for a beginner. While we were driving around the car park, Marcus rang to see how it was going and Sigmund went WILD because I answered the mobe. I said but it was ringing. He said YOU DON'T TALK ON THE PHONE while you're driving. I said was he blind? EVERYBODY talks on the phone while they're driving. He said well, they shouldn't. Especially if they can't drive. And then (despite his **PATHOLOGICAL** lack of interest in his youngest child) he suddenly remembered that I don't have a mobe and wanted to know where it came from. I said I bought it with the money I made in the summer, didn't I? Once he'd calmed down, I asked him when he thought I'd be ready to take to the road and he said as soon as I'd mastered only stopping when I mean to. The MC invited him in for tea when he brought me back!!! (I knew she'd soften once she got used to having him about again!) I left them alone, of course, but I did hear her ask him how it was going. He said about what you'd expect! Didn't I say I was a natural?

You'd think it'd be *easy* to return a pair of boots, wouldn't you? I mean you go to the shop, you give them the boots, and they give you your money back. Could anything be **SIMPLER**? Apparently the answer to that question is: **YES**—crossing the Channel in a washing-up bowl. You wouldn't believe the palaver! First of all, the sales assistant gave me this ginormous hard time because I'd lost the receipt. I said look at them—you know they came from here. He said he knew no such thing. He said they could've come from another shop on the road. I said, "But you were *here* when I bought them. Don't you remember? I was with a v tall boy with plaited hair." He said there was more than one v tall boy with plaited hair around here and he saw at least five of them a day. I said that he was being COMPLETELY unreasonable and that my stepfather was a solicitor so *I know my rights*. That convinced him! He said he wouldn't give me cash but I could exchange them for something else in the shop. Compromise is, of course, *très* important in Life, so I accepted this offer even though I'd rather have the dosh. Went to the back where they keep the clothes. I had a pair of black trousers with tons of pockets and zips in my hand and was debating whether or not I think corduroy's going to come back in when this bloke came up behind me and told me to get into the changing room. I said, "Hang on a minute! I haven't decided what I'm trying on yet!" He said, "NOW!!!" and gave me a poke. I said, "OI!" and turned around pretty sharply, of course. He was wearing a ski mask and POINTING A GUN AT ME! Then he said, "This is a holdup," just like in films. [Note to self: Does Art imitate Life, or is it the other way around?] There were three other girls in the shop and they were being herded to the changing rooms by another geezer in a ski mask. (God knows what thieves did before skiing became a popular sport!) As soon as we got in the changing room, the other girls started crying. I didn't see the point. I mean, it's not going to make the robbers change their minds, is it? The only effect crying hysterically might have is to annoy them so much they shoot you. And I really wanted to try on the black trousers. I don't think the robbery took too long. One minute I was surrounded by weeping women, and the next they were charging back into the shop to greet the police. I was grateful. It was way too crowded (and too distracting!) to really see what my bum looked like with that lot in there sobbing away. I was still studying myself in the mirror when someone started shouting through the curtain for me to come out. I said I was just in the middle of something. He said he was a police constable and he needed to take a statement. I said right, I'd only be a minute. He said, "NOW!" (He sounded just like the bloke with the gun.) So I never got to exchange the boots because the assistant was all involved with the cops. Took the boots home and stuck them at the back of my wardrobe. I don't seem to have much luck with boots. I wonder if that means something. Maybe I should ask Sappho.

*   *   *

I sat down with all Aunt K's new letters tonight to write her replies so I'm ready when the copy's due in next week. Of course, they're less **INSPIRING** than watching lettuce rot—weight, skin, jealous boyfriend, etc. (Once again I have to ask myself: Where's the *Passion*? Where's the **conflict**? Where's the blood and mud of **LIFE**?) I started to doze off. But just as sleep was trying to save me from terminal boredom, I was struck by yet another **BRILLIANT** idea for a problem that resonates with *Passion* and **conflict**! (I will admit that I probably wouldn't have thought of it if Rose Bandry the Thirteenth Disciple wasn't my grandmother. How can they say I never listen?) This beats the pants off Even After All He's Done Should I Take Him Back? (*Answer: NO! Give someone else a chance to ruin your life!*) Anyway, here's a **REAL** and excruciatingly dramatic problem—and it isn't anything that could wind up Mr. Cardogan either!

> *Dear Aunt Know-It-All,*
>
> *My brother just announced that he's gay. My father says that according to the Bible, homosexuality is an abomination and has thrown my brother out of the house. Is this true? Does this mean I shouldn't have anything to do with my brother either?*

Answer: Yes, it is true that *Leviticus* says homosexuality is an abomination. *Leviticus* says a lot of things: that anyone who consults the dead should be stoned to death and that only God can own land, and then there's a lot of detailed information about how to make animal sacrifices. I hope your father is making the proper blood offerings and growing a beard or he'll be in trouble even if he never speaks to your brother again. As for you, you have to make your own decision, but keep in mind that the Bible (though not *Leviticus*, of course) also has a lot to say about compassion and not judging others. If you do choose to join your father, I might know where you can get a nondefective goat.

TUESDAY 30 OCTOBER

Disha got tired of crying over Ethan in her room and came to the Body Shop with me today to help spend some of my birthday dosh. (Even Buskin' Bob can't have anything against Body Shop, so I'm safe there.) Ran into Lila, former best friend of Catriona Hendley! This was my chance to get the story firsthand. Asked Lila where the Hendley was. Lila said she didn't know because they weren't actually speaking to each other at the moment. I asked her what had happened. She said Catriona's pissed off because Lila borrowed a jacket of hers to take on holiday and never gave it back. I said oh, really? Then she went into a long saga of why she couldn't give it back (because she left it in San Francisco), why she couldn't replace it (it's irreplaceable), and why *she's* pissed off with Catriona (because Catriona's pissed off with her). I could tell she was making it up as she went along. When she finally stopped for air, I asked her what the name of the gym Catriona goes to was, as I was thinking of doing an aerobics course. Lila acted all bewildered and said she didn't know Catriona belonged to a gym. After Lila went off, I said to Disha, "**SEE**?" She said, "See what?" She said Lila told me exactly what she'd told *her*. I said but it isn't the truth. Disha said I only have my word for that. I said no sane people argue over a jacket, for God's sake. Disha said it's been known to happen. I said well, what about the gym? Disha asked if it had ever occurred to me that maybe Catriona **DOESN'T** belong to a gym? That maybe the letter in the paper wasn't about **HER**? I said now she sounded like David!

*   *   *

David came around this evening to help me study for my driving theory test. We wound up in **HELPLESS FITS OF LAUGHTER** because some of the multiple-choice answers were so stupid (e.g., What should you do before you set out in the fog?—b: Top up the radiator with antifreeze!). Also, I got a lot of the questions wrong. David said, "For God's sake, Janet, it's always the first answer." I said but that didn't always seem right to me. David said to think of the test like a school exam. They're not asking you to think, just to memorize the right answer. Buskin' Bob was watching the news (which, for Robert, is **NOT** a spectator sport—he actually talks back to the box!) when David was leaving. No sooner had the door shut behind David than Robert stopped arguing with the presenter to talk to me. He said, "So is David your boyfriend?" (God knows why he's obsessed with **MY** love life—you'd think he had enough to keep him busy with his own!) I said I'd already told him we were just good friends. He said we were laughing a lot. I said in my experience the sign of a relationship is when everybody *stops* laughing. Also, I think it's v immature to jump to conclusions like that.

WEDNESDAY 31 OCTOBER

Went to the zoo with Marcus today. Marcus doesn't like to go INTO the zoo because they're too much like jails— though their standards are higher than human jails, of course—but you can see quite a bit from outside. We both like the elephants best. We were strolling back talking about Life, etc., when who did I spy with my little eye but Queen Catriona. She said she couldn't stop to talk because she was meeting someone. I asked who. She said nobody I know and dashed off! I wanted to follow her. Marcus wanted to know why. I said so I could see who she was meeting. Marcus said, "Who cares who she's meeting?" I said I did—in case it was Mr. Plaget. Marcus said, "OK, I give up. Why would she be meeting Mr. Plaget?" I told him my theory. Marcus thought this was possibly the funniest joke I'd ever made. He said sometimes he thinks I have a really interesting mind and sometimes he just thinks I'm not really from this planet. He said Mr. Plaget has a girlfriend. I said it has been known for men to cheat on their girlfriends. Marcus said, "You haven't met Mr. Plaget's girlfriend, have you?" [Note to self: How is it possible that men, who are prone to violence and a love of power, etc., can be so trusting and gullible at the

198

same time?] By the time we finished this discussion, the
Hendley had vanished, of course. Marcus was relieved. He
didn't want to play spy; he wanted to get something to eat
since it'd been at least three hours since his last MAJOR
intake of food. So we headed for the high street. We were
just about to go into a café when I heard what sounded like
a sewing machine, and when I glanced around, Mr. Plaget's
Beetle went past. I punched Marcus and said, "Do you see
that? It's Mr. Plaget!" Marcus said, "So?" I said, "He's
obviously on his way to meet Catriona." Marcus said he was
going the wrong way. I'd never realized what a nitpicker
he was before. (It's just as well I don't really fancy him!)
Marcus said he'd decided that I *do* have an interesting mind,
but only because I'm totally in orbit.

The MC waited till I got back from the zoo to tell me that
Buskin' Bob and the Deadly Duo were coming around to
celebrate Halloween with us. I said not US—I'm going out.
(We're all going around to David's to watch horror videos
and eat black and orange food. Except Disha, of course.) The
MC said I wasn't going anywhere until I'd taken Marcella and
Lucrezia trick-or-treating! You could've knocked me over
with a small pumpkin! I said I really would recommend

hormonal treatment, as she's obviously lost the plot in a major way. She said that was nothing to what I was going to lose if I didn't do this. I said that frankly I was surprised Buskin' Bob would let his daughters go out begging for sweets when there were so many starving children in the world. The MC told me to put a sock in it. Then I said that since Marcella looks like she's going to be thirty on her next birthday, I didn't see why they needed me. The MC wasn't having any of it. She said she doesn't care how old Marcella looks; she's only eleven and there's no way she and Lucrezia are roaming around London on their own. Rang Marcus for support, since I reckoned David would be busy with the orange food coloring. Marcus said we should wear our *Matrix* costumes for a laugh. Marcella was dressed as Morgan le Fay (what else, right?) and Lucrezia was a unicorn. (Marcus was v admiring of her head, which, amazingly enough, Buskin' Bob made!) Since there are always tons of people in our neighborhood dressed in black and metal, I don't think anybody noticed that Marcus and I were in costume, but everybody noticed the Deadly Duo. (Heads **TURNED**!) Even though Marcella talked the whole time about her friends at school (yawn yawn!) and Lucrezia kept walking into things because she couldn't actually **SEE** out of the unicorn head, we had a good time because Marcus had us all laughing. (If I'm ever on 𝔇𝔢𝔞𝔱𝔥 ℜ𝔬𝔴 or something like that, I hope Marcus is with me, or at least that he's a regular visitor.) And the Deadly Duo made out like corporate executives. Even people who didn't know it was Halloween went scuttling off to find them something when they saw them. Marcus reckoned we should hit the goth hangout before we took them back because the goths are v into 𝔥𝔞𝔩𝔩𝔬𝔴𝔢𝔢𝔫 on a permanent basis. I said that was fine with me. Ms. Staples says you shouldn't rely on coincidence when you write fiction, but, if you ask me, LIFE is built on coincidence. We were just about to turn off the high street when I saw a couple with their arms wrapped around each other going into the trendy pub on the corner. I GASPED OUT LOUD!!! Marcus said, "Now what?" I said, "Look over there! That's the Wizard of Oz!" Marcus is an artist, so he has an eye for detail. Marcus said, "But that's not Disha. It looks like that waitress from Durango." It more than looked like her! It was Sky! I'd recognize that chest anywhere. Marcus said so, did Disha break up with the Wizard or something? I said not yet.

Was so distracted during the horror-film fest that I didn't scream ONCE! How could I? Reality is much more terrifying than any special effects. What are ghouls dripping ectoplasm and ax-wielding psychopaths compared to discovering that your best friend's boyfriend is a two-timing creep? Also, I was **TORN APART** by a Significant Moral Dilemma! Should I tell Disha about Ethan and Sky or not? I don't want her to be the **LAST** to find out, but on the other hand I don't want her to go into **DENIAL** (which Sigmund says is more common than the cold) and get angry with **ME**. David, Alice, and Siranee all agreed that Disha has a right to know if her boyfriend is two-timing her but they don't think I should say anything. I said but you just said she should know the truth!!! Alice said that was just the point— I don't know what the truth is. All I have is circumstantial evidence. I pointed out that **A LOT** of people have been electrocuted on circumstantial evidence, and Alice said but not in Britain. I then reminded them that I had more than circumstantial evidence—I had a **WITNESS**!!! But the pressure to conform is obviously more **POWERFUL** than the truth. Even though he'd seen **EXACTLY WHAT I SAW**, Marcus sided with the others! He said he knows how it *looked* but that doesn't mean that's how it *is*. It could have been completely innocent. I said but it could also have been completely **GUILTY**. Marcus said that's why he thinks I should have more proof before I get Disha all wound up. But it doesn't stop there! David insisted on walking me home. In case you think this was because he's concerned for my safety and would be devastated if I became a Crime Statistic, it wasn't. He wanted a Private Word! I said you mean you can't stand it anymore and want to confess your undying love for me? David laughed. He said he thought I should chill out on the Disha thing. He said, "You know what you're like, Janet!" I said, "No, what **AM I LIKE**?" He said I have the mind of a fiction writer, not a journalist. I said and what's wrong with that? David said I have a **TENDENCY** to jump to conclusions. Like with Worried Mate's letter. I said I didn't jump to conclusions with that; I deduced. He said well, I deduced **WRONG**. He happens to know who wrote that letter and it wasn't Lila. I said, "**OH, REALLY**? And how do you know that?" And he said, "**BECAUSE I WROTE IT!!!**" This time I laughed!!! I said and why would he do a thing like that? Apparently he was trying to **HELP ME**. Because I was so disappointed with the letters I was getting. I was practically struck dumb with shock and disbelief. I mean, just look at all the trouble he could've caused! (Perhaps David's not as *très*

203

intelligent as I thought!) I said that from now on if I
WANT his help, I'll be sure to ask him. I said also, that
doesn't change the fact that I SAW Ethan with another
woman, does it? The Eyes Don't Lie! David said the Eyes
Lie All the Time. He said he'd really like to visit my planet
sometime but he's not sure that he'd want to live there.

THURSDAY 1 NOVEMBER

Was still thinking about Disha when I went to bed. Tossed
and turned all night long on a mattress of **worry and care**.
Should I? Shouldn't I? Should I? Shouldn't I? Woke
up exhausted. To show you how ABSOLUTELY
DESPERATE I was, I actually brought it up over
breakfast. Marcella was still in bed and Lucrezia was
busy spreading organic butter on her toast (which takes
hours because it CAN'T touch the crust and has to be
completely even!), so I could actually get a few seconds of
attention. I said Aunt K had a letter from a girl who'd seen
her best friend's boyfriend with another girl and didn't
know what to do. I said since Buskin' Bob and the MC

were both pretty old, I reckoned they might have some worthwhile advice (for a change!). Buskin' Bob said it was a tricky problem (which was obviously **NEWS TO ME**). He said that just because you do something for a person's own good doesn't mean you're going to be thanked. Aside from the fact that I **DON'T ACTUALLY KNOW** what this girl saw (hah!!!), the friend could get more than she bargained for. Robert said that in ancient times they used to kill the bearer of bad news—which seems to me to be taking **DENIAL** a step too far! The MC was right behind him, of course. She wanted to know if I remembered the time Sigmund tried to help a woman who was being roughed up by her boyfriend at a bus stop and the two of them turned on him! (The answer to that question is: **NOT EVEN VAGUELY!**) I said so they were saying she shouldn't tell her? The MC said no, what they were saying was that Don't Know What to Do shouldn't jump in boots and all, the way I always do!!! She said Don't Know should be aware that she might get a black eye for her trouble. Even though I **KNOW WHAT I SAW**, all this **NEGATIVITY** shook my confidence a bit. [Note to self: Do humans have basically the same nature as cows—stay with the herd and go where they go? How have we ever made any progress?!!] Just in case I only *thought* I saw Ethan with Miss Bazooms, I asked Disha if she had a good time last night. D said in the end Ethan couldn't get off work so she watched some crap on the box on her own. I said she should've come over to David's. She said and how was she meant to talk to Ethan when he rang her after his shift? I said had she thought of using her mobe? She said she knows how much that irks me.

FRIDAY 2 NOVEMBER

The Hotspurettes **ARE STILL HERE**!!! I asked the MC when they were going home and she said **SUNDAY**. I said God knows why Buskin' Bob thinks he doesn't see enough of them—some of us see **FAR TOO MUCH**! The MC said they were staying for the Guy Fawkes party. I said what Guy Fawkes party? She said she'd told me. But she never did. The only things she tells *me* are what not to wear, eat, or wash my hair with. Apparently the whole clan's coming—Nan, Sigmund, even Mags and Sappho (even though Sappho has **ALWAYS REFUSED** to participate in Guy Fawkes before because she thinks it's barbaric to burn people in effigy—and also she thinks Guy Fawkes was set up and reckons it wouldn't necessarily have been such a bad thing if his plot had succeeded because at least it would've spared the country James I). I said well, what a shame that I wasn't going to be here for it, since I already had plans. She said to change them—Marcus can come around here instead. I said what made her think it was Marcus I had plans with and she said it was one of her wild guesses.

SATURDAY 3 NOVEMBER

Marcus didn't even flinch when I asked him about coming around here. (Unlike most artists, he doesn't shy away from family life.) He even turned up early because he didn't want to miss anything! (He needn't have worried.) All I can say is that if Guy Fawkes had had Lucrezia Hotspur on his team, the whole course of British history would've been different. You'd think a child who's afraid of rain and getting so much as a SMIDGEN of butter on the edge of her toast would be terrified of fireworks, but, sadly, that isn't the case. Lucrezia **LOVES** them. She loves them so much that while the rest of us were inside with the mulled wine (or fruit juice if you're Marcella or Sappho), she decided to start without us. It's amazing no one noticed she was gone (the lack of shrieking was a dead giveaway!). The first we knew anything was amiss was when Nan went to fetch the box of fireworks (she's always in charge because of her War Experiences) and she couldn't find them. Sigmund asked if she was sure she'd looked in the right place, but Buskin' Bob leaped to his feet like he was on springs, shouting, "**OH MY GOD**! Where's Lucrezia?" We got to the garden just in time to see Mr. Burl's garden shed go up like a rocket. (Fortunately Mr. Burl wasn't home.) Mags and Marcus got it out before the fire brigade had to be called. Marcus said that's what he loves about my family: there's never a dull moment. I said maybe not, but there are a lot of dull hours, days, weeks, months, and years.

SUNDAY 4 NOVEMBER

Sigmund took me for a drive this afternoon. (Or rather, I
TOOK HIM!!!) When we got in the car today, Sigmund
said that we were going to leave the block. I said, "Really?
You think I'm ready?" Desperate to convince me that he
does have a sense of humor, Sigmund said no, he was
beginning to doubt that I'll ever be truly ready, but he was
bored with driving in slow and dangerous circles for hours.
He said he reckoned we'd be safe enough if we kept to the
back streets. I admit that we got off to a bad start because I
didn't see the **NO ENTRY** sign (he was yammering away at
me, "Look! Indicate! Maneuver!"—I felt like I was in the
army!). So, of course, we went the wrong way up a one-
way road. He said, "BACK US OUT." I said, "I don't do
backwards." At first he was ADAMANT that I had to do
backwards, but he gave up that idea when I nearly hit the
BMW. So then we had to change places (which in a real car
is no big deal, of course, but in a Mini is like climbing out
of a tin), so he could back us out. After that, he was all
ATWITTER! Not only did he hang on to the dashboard
the whole time and yelp a lot, but he kept his legs straight
out as if he was trying to brake even though we were only

doing about five miles an hour because the back streets are one long speed bump. I told him he was making me nervous. How could he expect me to concentrate if he was going to undermine my confidence the whole time? I reminded him that this was exactly what happened when he was teaching the MC. From what I'd heard, he yelled at her even more than he yells at me. I said I would've thought a professional psychoanalyst would have more patience. I was still talking when Sigmund shouted, "JANET!" and grabbed the wheel. It's true that in times of stress (like when you're peacefully driving along and someone suddenly **BELLOWS** in your ear) your brain goes on automatic and your instincts take over. Because I was raised with Justin Bandry, who spent my childhood stealing my things, my instinct when someone tries to take something away from me is to hold on v tight. (This seems très reasonable to me.) Anyway, that's what I did. Sigmund pulled one way and I pulled the other. We hit a skip. Sigmund said he will *never* complain about speed bumps again. Think what could've happened if we'd been going any faster!

MONDAY 5 NOVEMBER

Another sleepless night of grappling with my Moral Dilemma.
I can forget about seeing Ethan and Sky for hours at a time in
daylight but as soon as I get into bed it comes back with a
VENGEANCE. Sigmund came in for a cuppa after his last
client, which is becoming a pretty regular event. He doesn't
even wait to be invited anymore. As per usual, he didn't
notice my anxious state (the dark circles of sleeplessness . . .
the pale complexion of moral torment). I was tempted to ask
him what *he* thought about Don't Know's problem but
changed my mind since being a Cheater himself he might be
prejudiced in Ethan's favour. (I know he's meant to be an
Objective Professional, but birds of a feather DO flock
together, don't they?) So instead I asked him if he thinks that
humans are ruled by the herd instinct. He said yes. Sigmund
says that humans have made progress more or less in spite of
themselves. He says that change has come about because one
or two visionaries have had the courage to challenge the
established ideas of their times—and have usually ended up
imprisoned, murdered, or branded heretics for their trouble.
I said if he was trying to comfort me, he hadn't succeeded.
He wanted to know if we had any biscuits.

WEDNESDAY 7 NOVEMBER

Yet another night of turning and tossing and troubled dreams.
(In one I was waiting for a bus with a herd of cows when
suddenly one of them turned into Disha and decked me!)
Should I? Shouldn't I? Should I? Shouldn't I? Sigmund's always
banging on about dreams being the subconscious mind trying
to work out problems, and for once I think he may be on to
something. When I woke up this morning I finally had the
solution to my soul-ripping problem: write to Aunt K! Then
when the letter comes out, I'll show it to Disha and see what
she thinks. *What would* YOU *do, Disha? Would you tell her or not?*
Whatever D says is what I'll do! This way I can't possibly make
a mistake. Aunt K's reply was easy (*Your friend already has one person
close to her who's lying—don't make it two!*), but it took me a while
to get Don't Know What to Do's letter right so that she seems
sympathetic and not interfering. Was nearly late for school
again. Handed in my copy to Ms. Staples. She wanted to know
when I was going to write a feature piece for the magazine. I
said what with my academic work, my social life, my emotional
growth, AND sorting out everyone else's problems, I
really haven't been able to fit it in. It's astounding to me that
the Prime Minister ever has time to practice his guitar!

THURSDAY 8 NOVEMBER

D invited me around to hers after school. She and Ethan
have had another fight (now, there's a change!). Disha
said it was all her fault—she was annoyed because they
were meant to hang out on Saturday and he couldn't make
it after all. I said well, maybe she had a **RIGHT** to be
annoyed. After all, they'd made plans, hadn't they? Disha
said it wasn't Ethan's fault if he had to work, was it?
I said I thought he was a waiter, not a policeman. Also,
MAN DOES NOT LIVE BY BREAD ALONE.
Disha said try telling that to the Ethiopians. Disha said she
doesn't feel it's right that she gets fed up with Ethan's
work schedule—esp. when she knows there's nothing he
can do about it. Apparently loving someone else should
make you less selfish and très more *Thoughtful and
Understanding*. I said, "You mean like the way Ethan's
so amazingly *Thoughtful and Understanding* of you?"
She said I didn't know what I was talking about since I'd
never been in *Love*. I said well, maybe I'm not the only
one who doesn't know what she's talking about!

FRIDAY 9 NOVEMBER

Decided to veg out in front of the box while the MC was fixing supper. (As you know, I'm not really a telly person—especially since it's all reality TV nowadays. I like a little more intellectual stimulation than watching a bunch of people in a house annoy each other—I get enough of that in my daily life—but this is such a strenuous and demanding term that sometimes I need to MINDLESSLY RELAX.) Was so whacked that though I don't usually watch the news because it's SO depressing—no wonder Buskin' Bob sings about dead hobos; it's almost light relief!!!—I didn't even have the strength to lift the remote and on it came. There was an award-winningly boring interview with some bloke from the government [Note to self: Why do politicians NEVER answer the question they're asked—even if it's repeated several times?], so I drifted off. I was thinking about Life and staring at the screen when I realized I was watching some fanatical protest types having a scuffle with the police. One of the fanatics looked familiar. I turned up the sound. A bunch of people had climbed over a fence at an air base and hung up an antiwar banner. The woman being hauled off by the

214

coppers was Nan!!! I yelled for the Mad Cow. She didn't
seem v taken aback to see her mother-in-law being nicked.
She said Nan's arthritis doesn't seem to be giving her any
trouble, does it?

SATURDAY 10 NOVEMBER

Sigmund came to take me for another driving lesson.
Found him in the kitchen drinking tea and eating chocolate
biscuits with the MC. The two of them were laughing like
hyenas about Nan's run-in with the LAW. Sigmund said
he never expected to be putting up bail for his mother. It
was meant to be angry young men who wound up in jail,
not angry old women. I said, "Welcome to the twenty-first
century."

I was doing really well with my driving today when all of
a sudden we turned this corner. I said that's a roundabout
up ahead. Sigmund said I was one hundred percent correct
and to take the right-hand lane. He said it was gratifying
for him to discover that the education system hasn't failed

me like it has so many others. I said, "But I don't do roundabouts." He said, "You do now." He said the important thing was not to panic. Just remember what he told me. I didn't see how I could do that when I had **NO RECOLLECTION** of him telling me anything, but I said I'd try. Got onto the roundabout without too much trouble (Sigmund did a bit of yelping but the other driver didn't beep his horn or shake his fist or anything of that ilk, so it was just Sigmund overreacting as usual), but then I couldn't get off it! It was really surreal. We just went around and around and around. Sigmund was yelling that I had to move left but I couldn't move left because there were already all these cars there. They just kept coming like they were on some berserk assembly line. I was actually **DIZZY** by the time I finally made a break for it. (And you should've heard all the horns honking then!)

No sign of Buskin' Bob at all this weekend! And today when we got back from my lesson the MC asked Sigmund if he wanted to stay for supper. Sigmund said yes. He said he felt as if he'd just crossed the Atlantic on a raft pursued by sharks and needed some adult company (which seemed to mean the MC!). She made his favorite: macaroni cheese with crushed crisps on top. He's never really grown up, if you ask me. I reckon that Peter Pan probably lived on macaroni cheese and chocolate biscuits too! (But without the white wine and fags.) I wonder if anyone's ever done a scientific study on the relationship between food preferences and emotional maturity. (One of my favorite foods is smoked salmon, of course!) Just to prove that **CHANGE** really is the nature of the universe, we had a v pleasant family meal with no singing or lectures on **Corporate Greed**.

WEDNESDAY 14 NOVEMBER

Forget Thorpe Park. If you want a real white-knuckle ride, *Love* is obviously the thrill of choice. Disha's roller coaster is swinging madly among the clouds again. She was brighter than a spotlight today because she and the Wizard are back on. It's no wonder her brain has turned to slush; she must be exhausted from all the toing and froing. [Note to self: Is *Love* anything more than a faulty light switch in the electrics of the heart?] Disha said the good bits are more than worth the bad bits. Also, what can she do—she's in *Love*? I said I

217

didn't realize it was meant to be a terminal disease. I said she sounds like one of those old American blues songs sung by a woman who's going to end up with a broken heart as well as a few broken bones. Disha thought I was joking. She said she prefers the love songs about being complete and blissed out and never having any meaning in your life before you met him. I said I didn't see how a **VIRTUAL STRANGER** could do all that. (Esp. one who has hairy ears!) I said if she hadn't met Ethan, she would've met someone else and be saying the same things about **HIM**. Disha said I'm wrong! She said she would probably have gone her whole life without ever *Falling in Love*. I said I couldn't believe that the survival of the species depended on a chance meeting like that. If it did, there'd probably only be about six humans alive and they'd all look alike and need help getting out of the rain. Disha said what about all those women after the World Wars who always remained true to the soldiers they loved who never came back? I said I reckoned that after a World War, they wouldn't have had much choice, considering how few soldiers actually did come back. I said what about *Sleepless in Seattle*? Tom Hanks finds *True Love* twice. D said that some people's destiny includes two *Loves of Your Life*—but not hers.

THURSDAY 15 NOVEMBER

David says it's ironic that I can sort out everybody's problems but Disha's. I said I thought it would probably help if Disha realized she *has* a problem.

SATURDAY 17 NOVEMBER

Today's driving lesson was cut short by a flat tire. First Sigmund went mad because I didn't realize we had a puncture and kept driving. I said I thought he wanted me to concentrate on getting down the road without hitting anything. Also, how was I meant to know we had a puncture when the only smooth ride in the Mini is when you're parked? Then he went mad because he had to take the bottles out of the boot to get to the jack. Sigmund said it doesn't count as recycling if you never actually take them to the bottle bank. I said not to tell me; I was just the child. Then he had another fit because the jack wasn't in the boot. I said the MC moved it to make room for the bottles (which was true except for the bit about the MC, since she doesn't do *anything* if she can get me to do it, but I don't see why I should take the blame—I'm completely in favor of just throwing the bottles in the bin like we used to!). As soon as we got back to the **House of Horror**, he started yelling at the MC about the jack and the bottles, etc. It really was like old times. If Justin had been there grunting and pawing the ground, I'd've thought I'd been dreaming the whole separation. Went to my room for some peace and quiet.

SUNDAY 18 NOVEMBER

Apparently Sigmund woke up this morning knowing that today was the day I should learn to park. I said I knew how to park; you just pulled into the space. He said he meant *parallel* parking. I said I never intended to use it. He said I might have to. All I can say is **LET'S HOPE NOT**!!! He made me drive all the way to Dollis Hill because the streets are wider and not as busy as around ours. If you ask me, they put the curb too close to the road. It's virtually impossible not to hit it or go over it. Was **TOTALLY**

SHATTERED by the time I finally got into the space, what with all the yelling and screaming (and clinking of the bottles in the boot). Sigmund wanted to know how I could be seventeen and not know the difference between PARALLEL and PERPENDICULAR. I said I did know the difference but I didn't think it really mattered with the Mini since it hardly sticks out at all. He said he can't wait till I get to hill starts. He said perhaps in the future we should bring the mobe with us after all so I'll be able to ring for the ambulance when he has a heart attack.

Despite yesterday's argument about the recycling, it looks to me like my little plan is working très brilliantly. As soon as we got back to the House of Horror, Sigmund went straight into the kitchen for yet another cup of tea!!! The MC didn't bat an eyelid! She said, "Bad Day at Black Rock?" Sigmund said teaching me to drive made the Gunfight at the OK Corral look like a church picnic. I laughed too. I do feel it's important for them to have their little jokes if they're going to patch things up.

TUESDAY 20 NOVEMBER

Mr. Belakis kept the art room open after class so Marcus
and I worked on our art projects all afternoon. I was going
to do one of those traditional portraits with everyone
posed in their good clothes, but though my family
members don't think very much, they do move about a
lot, so I'm making it more active. Marcus was v impressed
with my depiction of Nan lobbing the balloon at the police
van. We got so absorbed in our work that the only three
cars left in the car park when Mr. Belakis finally threw us
out were Mr. Belakis's Volvo, Mr. Plaget's Beetle, and Mr.
Tulliver's Kawasaki. Ran into Catriona on the way out.
Even though nobody asked her, she insisted on telling us
how she'd had to stay late to work on the magazine
AGAIN. Apparently the job of Editor-in-Chief is
NEVER DONE. She said I must be deliriously happy
that I'm just a feature writer — or will be if I ever write a
feature. I said I was. I said I feel there are **FAR MORE**
important things in life than correcting punctuation.

SUNDAY 25 NOVEMBER

Since Marcus is about to start the part of his painting where his grandparents come to England, he wanted to check out the light on a rainy autumn afternoon, so we went to the park. Apparently his grandparents used to hang out there when they first came over because the trees reminded them of home. (Either my image of Jamaica is COMPLETELY wrong or Marcus's grandparents were v lonely!) Ran into Mr. Plaget under an umbrella. We would've walked right past him but I recognized his ratty old sneakers (mathematicians don't care about their appearance—Einstein used to turn up for important dinners in his pajamas). The Beetle had broken down and he was taking a shortcut home. Marcus wanted to know if I didn't think that was a little odd. I said not at all. Our car was as old as Mr. Plaget's and it was ALWAYS breaking down. Marcus said not *that*—the fact that Mr. Plaget was walking home instead of ringing the RAC. I said I thought that was pretty rich coming from him since he's always telling ME not to leap to the wrong conclusion. I said there could be a dozen reasons why he was walking. Marcus said he'd buy me a coffee if I could name even five. I had a mocha latte.

FRIDAY 30 NOVEMBER

It's been one of those six-of-one, half-a-dozen-of-the-other days (and which days aren't, right?). The first part was très brilliant. The second issue of the mag sold out by lunchtime. EVERYBODY was talking about Aunt K. Even Old Woolly Jumper gave me a knowing smile when I passed him in the corridor. That and the ASTOUNDING progress the Old Folks Not Quite at Home are making (no Buskin' Bob ALL WEEK!) have certainly shown those naysayers like my mother, who didn't think I was a gifted problem solver! It wasn't until the afternoon that the day sort of fell apart. As you can imagine, I was feeling v confident with all the positive feedback. Read out the letter from Don't Know What to Do to Disha at lunch. I said I thought it was a tricky situation. What would she do? Disha said she'd tell her. (She said this with NO HESITATION!) She said it was the duty of a *Best Friend* to tell the truth— esp. about something like that. So I told her about seeing Ethan with Miss Bazooms on Halloween. Did she fall into my arms sobbing with gratitude? Did she cry out OH, THANK GOD, AT LAST I KNOW THE HORRID TRUTH? Did she thank me for being the *Best Friend* a girl ever had? **NO, SHE DID NOT**!!! She went **COMPLETELY MAD**!!! First she was pissed off because I'd taken so long to tell her!!! She said she supposed I'd told everyone else I know and we were all laughing at her behind her back. And then she was pissed off because I'd told her at all. She said that at best I hadn't seen what I had seen—that I'd **LEAPED TO THE WRONG CONCLUSION AS PER USUAL**—and that at worst I was making it up because I'm jealous of her happiness. I said what happiness would that be? She was usually depressed. She said I should mind my own business **FOR A CHANGE**! She said hadn't I learned my lesson from my mistake about Catriona and Mr. Plaget? (I knew I shouldn't've told her about David writing the letter. She's always been a very **TOLD-YOU-SO** sort of person.) I said this was different. She said it wasn't. She said I've been trying to throw a spanner in the works ever since she started seeing Ethan! I said I had not. Also, I wasn't the only one who saw them. Marcus, Marcella, and Lucrezia saw them too. She said and that means what? She said Marcella's self-obsessed, Lucrezia's on drugs, and Marcus would say anything I told him to say. I said he would not (I couldn't really argue with the other two objections). I said I was sorry—I was only trying to help. After all, it's my duty as a *Best Friend*, isn't it? Disha accepted my apology, but after that the atmosphere was a bit like Frosty the Snowman BEFORE the thaw. Decided to go around to Disha's after school to patch things up. (I can see now, of course, that I should've left well enough alone. But I didn't.) Ran into David and Marcus on the way and they invited themselves along. I reckoned she'd be nicer to me if they were there, so I didn't argue. Mrs. Paski was just going out when we got there. She said Disha and Ethan were in the kitchen and told us to go on through. You'd think I'd turned up with a herd of wildebeests from the expression on D's face, but Ethan acted like we were long-lost friends. *Oh, Janet, it's been ages. . . . Oh, David and Marcus, I've heard so much about you. . . .* So it was all blah blah blah until Disha started dropping hints that they wanted to be alone. As soon as we got outside, David and Marcus had a go AT ME, of course!!! They said Ethan seemed like a nice bloke. David said didn't I say you were overreacting? Got so embroiled in this conversation that we were at the corner before I realized I'd left my schoolbag in Disha's kitchen. Ran back to get it but I only got as far as the front door. There was such an almighty ROW going on inside that for a second I thought I'd stepped back in

226

time and was listening to Sigmund and the MC! It was Ethan mainly. He was all **INCENSED** that there was something going on between Disha and **MARCUS**!!! Or maybe Disha and **DAVID**!!! Or maybe Disha and **BOTH OF THEM**!!! I don't know if it's me, but **JUST** when I think I know how peculiar people can be, they get worse. Then the **PENNY FINALLY DROPPED**! This explains everything! Why Disha and Ethan never hang out with the rest of us . . . why she didn't come to my party . . . why she ran off that time we were having coffee with the lads because Ethan walked by, and then they had another fight . . . **HOW COULD I HAVE BEEN SO BLIND**? It was right there in front of me all the time and I didn't see it!!! Sigmund was **WRONG** (as per usual). It isn't Disha who's **jealous and possessive**—it's the Wizard of Oz! [Note to self: People often accuse innocent others of doing what they're doing themselves—i.e., Ethan being jealous of Disha when all the time he was the one who was cheating. Is this to divert attention from themselves or is it because they assume everyone else is just as bad as they are?] **I WAS TOTALLY GOBSMACKED**! I just stood there with my jaw hanging like a chandelier. I felt like I'd been superglued to the Paskis' front step. But not for long!!! I was still trying

227

to **ABSORB** everything I'd heard when the door started to open (Ethan's voice may carry over miles but his footsteps are silent as a moth's!). It's a bloody good thing that I'm used to thinking on my feet, that's all I can say! I was in Mrs. Paski's herbaceous border faster than a flea on a cat! Ethan slammed the door behind him (so anyone who'd missed his shrieking would know he was angry) and strode down the path. I wasn't breathing but I was praying. I reminded God that my Nan is a v close friend of His and begged Him to make Ethan go in the opposite direction to Marcus and David. For once, He was listening! The first thing the lads said when I got back to them was, "Why have you got leaves in your hair?" The second was, "**SO WHERE'S YOUR BAG**?" I said it was a **Hostage to Love**!

Tried ringing Disha when I got home but her mobe was off and no one answered the landline. I kept calling, "Disha! Disha! It's **ME**!" on the answering machine but she wouldn't pick up. All I got was Mr. Paski's voice telling me to please leave a message and someone would ring me back as soon as possible. I suppose she could've suddenly had to go to Moscow or been kidnapped by pirates because D *didn't ring back.* I left six messages and then gave up. (It makes you think about progress, doesn't it? Here we are at the pinnacle of civilization and all it means is that you get to humiliate yourself by leaving messages for someone who's probably standing right there staring at the answering machine while pretending to be too busy to talk to you!) This is what happens when you listen to others!!! If I'd told Disha what I knew about Ethan right off, I could at least have saved her a couple more weeks of needless **suffering**. But OH, NO— I succumbed to peer pressure like everyone else. Have been in a deep and reflective mood all night. I can't believe that all this **drama and trauma** has been going on for months and Disha didn't tell me! I'm her *Best Friend*!!! She's always told me EVERYTHING!!! And when I say EVERYTHING, I mean EVERYTHING! (Who was the person she rang when the string broke on the tampon that time? That's right, it was Janet Bandry!) I feel like we're in a play together, but we're working from different scripts.

Marcus just rang to see if I'd talked to Disha. I said she doesn't seem to want to talk to me! He said I shouldn't take it personally. After all, she just had a MAJOR fight with her boyfriend so she's probably too upset to talk to anyone. I said she's always just had a major fight with her boyfriend.

119

Also, **I'M HER BEST MATE**! Marcus said people in *Love* don't have best mates until *after* the relationship's over (which even in my distraught state I thought was a très profound thing to say—must remember it for Aunt K!).

SATURDAY 1 DECEMBER

Woke up with a **GINORMOUS** sense of responsibility re Disha. I felt it was time we had a **SERIOUS** conversation about her and Ethan. I had to make her see that Ethan's jealousy doesn't mean that he loves her—it just means he's **jealous**. Also, she's obviously in desperate need of some female support. Didn't even ring to tell her I was coming to collect my schoolbag, but just turned up at her door. Mrs. Paski said that D was still in bed but it was about time she rose to greet the day and I should go up. Disha was dressed but lying on her bed as if it was made of nails, smoking a cigarette. She was all red-eyed and gloomy (for a change!). I said if she didn't stop puffing away like a chimney in winter, she's going to have a lot more to worry about than just love, and she gave me this **UGLY** look and said,

"WHAT DO YOU WANT? HAVEN'T YOU DONE ENOUGH ALREADY?" I said, "What's that supposed to mean?" She said, "Bringing Marcus and David around like that when you knew it was a Friday and Ethan would be there." I said I had forgotten about that (which was TRUE!). I said and anyway, I didn't think it would be a big deal since I'd HAD NO IDEA that the reason she never brought Ethan around was because he's jealous and possessive. Disha said, "WHAT MAKES YOU SAY THAT?!!" (IT ABSOLUTELY DEFIES BELIEF!!!) I told her what made me say that. I said that since I'd heard them arguing yesterday I'd been v worried about her. I said it sounded to me like Ethan has some unresolved issues (as in *he's out of his mind*). She said so now I was an EAVESDROPPER as well! (I didn't ask as well as what?!!) I said I wasn't eaves-dropping; the way they were screaming, I would've heard them in Iceland. We went back and forth like a tennis ball at Wimbledon and then she TOLD ME TO LEAVE! She said she never wants to speak to me again EVER—not even if we're reincarnated as giraffes a thousand years from now and I know where the best trees are. Came home and cried all afternoon! This is the most MEGA fight we've had since I lost her brown velvet shirt when we were fourteen.

SUNDAY 2 DECEMBER

Have been in a funk **ALL DAY**. Only left my room to
eat and get a cup of tea, etc. Every time the phone went, I
thought it might be Disha ringing to apologize but it never
was. I'm beginning to understand why Sigmund's not better
at his job. I mean, he really couldn't be, could he? People
are a lot less predictable than the random movements of the
cosmos. You have more chance of winning the lottery than
understanding your *Very Best Friend in the World*.

MONDAY 3 DECEMBER

Despite the fact that I'm taking a break from the Dark
Phase, if my life gets any darker, I'm going to have to
walk around wearing one of those miner's helmets so I
can see where I'm going. Disha **DISSED** me so
completely today that I almost thought she'd suddenly
gone blind (which I suppose she has — though not *literally*,
of course). Hi, *Marcus* . . . Hi, *David* . . . Hi, *Total Stranger That
I've Never Spoken to Before* . . . She didn't even come to lunch.

234

She told David she was on a diet and was going to spend lunch period in the library feeding her mind instead! (She'll be behind the bike shed stuffing her sarnies into her face more like!) It's not so much the silent treatment as the nothing-at-all treatment. I have ceased to exist. I put a brave face on it, of course, and acted like I didn't notice (and that if I did notice, I wouldn't care), but inside, a **dank, chill wind** was howling through my heart and soul. It's only the knowledge that I'm **RIGHT** that got me through the day.

WEDNESDAY 5 DECEMBER

Day Three of Nothing at All. Waiting for Disha to come around is obviously like waiting for a 46 bus in a storm. Only with Disha I can't just walk home; I'm stuck here with rain dripping down my neck and soaking into my shoes.

THURSDAY 6 DECEMBER

Too depressed even to open Aunt K's post. I mean, what's
the point? Maybe Mr. Cardogan was right and there's a lot
to be said for spots and fat thighs. At least there are things
you can do about physical problems (i.e., eat fresh fruit and
vegetables and have liposuction) but I'm beginning to think
that the only good advice about personal relationships you
can give anyone is: **Abandon hope, all who enter here**!!! Either
that or **GET A DOG**.

FRIDAY 7 DECEMBER

Not even a pile of letters for Aunt K could cheer me up
today. Ms. Staples was with me when I picked up Aunt K's
post and she noticed that I stuffed it in my bag without
even counting it. She wanted to know if something was
wrong—I've seemed moody and distracted all week.
I said it was just Life. She said that sounded like a Bob
Dylan line. (My God! Things are worse than I thought if
I'm quoting Bob Dylan!) I said well, he is something of a

poet, isn't he? I said I reckon it's a bit like Great Minds thinking alike—you know, poets think alike too. She said she still hasn't read my poems. Well, how could she? I haven't written them yet. (But you do have to admire Ms. Staples's memory. It's *months* since I mentioned the poems. You'd think someone over thirty would've forgotten it by now.)

SATURDAY 8 DECEMBER

There's nothing like driving around the back streets of north London with an unstable psychotherapist to take your mind off your problems. *Clutch . . . Brake . . . Faster . . . Slower . . . Watch out for that . . . Watch out for this . . . Signal, Janet. Signal, Janet . . . Janet, the gears . . . No, not the bloody windscreen wipers!!!* He just never stops! And I was **DEFINITELY** not in the mood for it today! I mean, I'm doing my best, but there's a lot to remember. It's not as if I don't have a **LIFE**! Also, it wasn't as if I was making **GINORMOUS** mistakes. They were all really piddly (signal right, turn left, etc.). Then this motorbike nearly plowed into us (they really do come out of **NOWHERE**!). Both Sigmund and the rider lost it completely. Sigmund was screaming at me on one side and 𝕯𝖆𝖗𝖙𝖍 𝖁𝖆𝖉𝖊𝖗 was shrieking on the other. Neither of them would calm down, so I got out of the car and left them to it. Had to walk home since I wasn't about to go back and ask Sigmund for the bus fare. The MC wanted to know where he was. I said back on Camden Road as far as I knew. He turned up eventually. My Father the Role Model said that if he had an addictive personality, he'd probably be shooting up heroin by now (and they wonder why I can be a bit dramatic at times—where do they think I get it from?). I said he does have an addictive personality—he's hooked on cigarettes, isn't he? He banged his head on the fridge. The upshot is that he **REFUSES** to give me any more lessons! I ask you, what sort of example is that meant to be for me, just quitting like that? But, as I've said before, Life isn't all one thing or another. Stomped off to my room to recover from this trauma. Decided **ANEW** that **I NEVER WANT TO BE LIKE MY PARENTS**. I mean really. No wonder Sigmund's stuck in Kilburn on an army cot, with his attitude. Decided that though there's nothing I can do about the small earlobes, that doesn't mean I also have to inherit Sigmund's lack of fortitude and determination. Decided I would **FORCE** myself to write Aunt K's replies to the more practical problems at least and went back to the kitchen for my schoolbag. Arrived just in time to hear the MC invite Sigmund around for Christmas!!! Sigmund said what about the other Mrs. Bandry and the MC said of course Nan was invited; it wouldn't be Christmas without her. Despite the fact that "it wouldn't be Christmas without Nan" translates as "it wouldn't be Christmas without a major fight between Sigmund and Nan," I couldn't help feeling pretty chuffed about this. Obviously things are going the way I intended between the parents! Set to work on Aunt K's column with new enthusiasm. Wrote myself another letter about Disha and signed it I Was Only Trying to Help.

SUNDAY 9 DECEMBER

Sappho turned up this afternoon with a suitcase. I said
don't tell me Mags threw you out; I didn't know that
happened in same-sex couples. Sappho said *everything*
happens in same-sex couples, including arguments over
who never fills the ice-cube trays, but that she hasn't been
given the old heave-ho. Mags's mother is v ill, so she had
to go up north to be with her. I said so you decided to
move in with us because you're afraid if you fall on your
back while you're on your own, you won't be able to get
up again? As per usual, I laughed alone. The MC said just
wait till I'm pregnant and see how funny I think it is. As
I'm v discouraged about even *Falling in Love* at this point,
I told her it could be a long wait. Apparently there are a
lot of things Sappho can't do around the house because of
her ginormous size and all her aches and pains—and Mags
doesn't want her to be on her own in case the baby is
early. Then they sprung the REALLY BIG surprise on
me. Sappho's having my room! I said why couldn't she kip
in Justin's, and the MC said because Justin only has the
futon and not a bed, and we couldn't expect Sappho to
sleep on that (which isn't true, of course—I could expect

her to). So I had to move into the Black Hole of Wooster Crescent. It took me all afternoon just to make some room for my stuff and get rid of the boy stink (apparently not noticed by the Deadly Duo—probably because Marcella was talking too much and Lucrezia was shrieking).

MONDAY 10 DECEMBER

When I finally get around to writing the Story of My Life (after I've lived it a bit more), this part is going to be called **Janet Bandry and the Chamber of Horrors**! I swear to God, Geek Boy's room is **haunted**! I couldn't sleep because I was worrying what's going to happen when the Mad Cow is really old and needs someone to look after her. (I hope she's not expecting me to drop my life and rush to her side like Mags. Not after the way she treats me!) Anyway, because I was awake, I heard all these weird sounds. I **KNOW** I heard groaning and creaking and am extremely certain that I heard chains rattling as well! (I almost feel that I should've expected this, since if anyone fits the description of **The Unquiet Dead**, it's my brother.) The MC says it's all in my mind. I pointed out that I never hear strange sounds in my room. Also, the **Chamber** still reeks in a v unnatural way. The MC says it's just the darkroom. Well, that's all right then. It isn't the smell of **terror and doom**—it's the smell of poison in the air! The MC wanted to know if I thought I was ever going to grow out of over-dramatizing everything. I said probably soon—when I die an **ugly and tragic death**, suffocated by toxic wastes.

TUESDAY 11 DECEMBER

Another night in the **Chamber of Horrors**! (If I end up dropping out of school and becoming a government statistic, we all know **WHO'S TO BLAME!**) Woke up to the sound of stealthy footsteps and the mournful moans of a restless soul in endless pain. Any ordinary person would have pulled the duvet over her head très rapidly, but not I! I decided to prove to the Mad Cow that the ghost wasn't in my mind, but in our flat. I switched on the reading lamp over the futon and leaped into action.

For the first time in my young life I was glad my brother is as far from normal as the Earth is from Jupiter. Normal people have makeup and books and stuffed animals, etc., in their rooms, but Geek Boy's got cameras! I grabbed the one on top of the chest of drawers, turned the light off again and made for the door. I expected to see the eerie glow of a troubled spirit, but the hall was dark. **THOUGH NOT SILENT**!!! I could hear the low moans of perpetual torment coming from the linen cupboard. I'm not saying I wasn't frightened; my heart was pounding like an oil pump! But Life is frightening, isn't it? You never know what's going to happen next— and I've experienced enough to know that there's no reason to expect that whatever it is will be **GOOD**. But I believe that you can't **TRULY LIVE** if you don't take chances. (If you can be mown down by hired killers while you're watching cricket, then there's really nothing to stop you going after a ghost, is there?) I tiptoed down the hall. I stopped at the linen cupboard. I raised my camera. I yanked open the door and pressed the button in one brave motion. There was a flash of light. Sappho, who was sitting on the toilet with her head in her hands, looked up pretty sharply and screamed. To her credit, she

241

took the whole incident a lot better than the MC. Sappho thought it was pretty funny. Also, she understood that since I wasn't used to sleeping in Geek Boy's room, I was understandably confused about which door was the linen cupboard and which was the bathroom. The Mad Cow said that as I've lived in the flat since I was four she reckons I should know that much. I said it isn't my fault that I'm not in my own room. Also, who expects anyone to be roaming around the flat in the dead of night, moaning? The MC said it was lucky for me there was no film in the camera. She said wait till Robert and your father hear this one!

WEDNESDAY 12 DECEMBER

I always thought you're meant to glow when you're pregnant because you're fulfilling your Biological Destiny, but it turns out this is yet another myth. Sappho walks around like her arms are on backwards, and her skin's the color of Buskin' Bob's organic soya milk. If you ask me, she looks like she's fulfilling that other Great Biological

Destiny—dying. I said was she sure this pregnancy's **NORMAL**? I've heard of women taking off ten minutes from plowing a field to have a baby then going straight back to work, but Sappho's exhausted just walking to the bathroom (where she spends an inordinate amount of time, if you ask me). Sappho said there is no such thing as normal for everyone—just normal for **YOU**. Apparently Sappho has a friend who went to the hospital with acute stomach pains and came back with a seven-pound son—and she'd never even known she was knocked up! I said well, Life is **JUST FULL OF SURPRISES**, isn't it?

The only person to appreciate my courage and intrepidity in pursuing the ghost without a thought to my own personal safety is Nan. Nan said I would've been useful in the war as a **SPY**! Sigmund said only if I'd been working for the Germans.

THURSDAY 13 DECEMBER

At last something good has happened to me!!! Justin's
NOT COMING HOME!!! Well, not yet at any rate.
God knows, no one told me he was meant to come back in
December, but today the Mad Cow had a postcard from
him saying he's having such a brilliant time among the
poor of hungry Mexico that he's staying on. I can't tell you
what a relief this is. I've still got some of Geek Boy's ill-
gotten gains but not so little that he wouldn't notice
there's a bit missing if he came back now.

It's just as well Disha's not speaking to me because it would
cost me a bomb on the mobe since Mags and Sappho talk on
the landline every night and it goes on for hours (maybe
Sappho's right about lesbians being no different from
straight women!). Apparently Mags's mum isn't making a
miraculous recovery. The Mad Cow and Sappho were talking
about what might happen (as in, maybe the old lady's going
to that Great Bingo Hall in the Sky), and Sappho said at least
her will is all in order. Can't help wondering if the MC's will
is in order. What if it isn't? What if she leaves everything to
Justin? I just hope I don't get the car.

FRIDAY 14 DECEMBER

This afternoon I casually remarked to the MC that the flat was going to be a bit crowded over Christmas, what with Sappho staying and all. The MC said she feels that at Christmas it's a case of the More the Merrier (which is not something she's ever thought before!!!). Apparently she's worked it all out: Sappho and Nan can have the double bed in her room, I can have my room, the Deadly Duo can sleep on their air beds on **MY FLOOR**, Sigmund can sleep in Justin's room, and she and Robert will take the sofa. I said **PARDON**? I said when did the Hotspurs get back in the frame? The MC said as far as she knew, they were never out of it. I said well, I hadn't heard any catchy tunes about dead hobos being played in the flat recently. The MC said that was because Robert's been away with work. She said it as though I should've already known this, which, of course, I didn't. She said where did I think that postcard on the fridge from Malaysia came from? I said Malaysia obviously (though to be **ABSOLUTELY** honest I never looked at it twice—I reckoned it was from Geek Boy). Then she started laughing. She wanted to know if I'd thought she and the Eco Warrior had broken up. I said

well, it had occurred to me as a possibility. I said Sigmund
had been around quite a bit lately, hadn't he? She said
Sigmund has always been around quite a bit. She said the
only person who stopped speaking to him for a while was
ME. She says she doesn't want to ban him from her life;
she just doesn't want to live with him anymore. I said I still
think it's a bit much having him stay here with her new
boyfriend. It won't be v comfortable for him. She
said Sigmund doesn't mind—he likes Robert. Then
ANOTHER DASTARDLY thought occurred to me.
I asked if this meant I was supposed to buy presents for
Robert AND the Deadly Duo too? The MC wanted to
know if it was just *her* I don't listen to or if it was
everybody. I said it was just her. She said I was there when
we all decided to have an Oxford Christmas this year. As
per usual, I had no idea what she was on about. I said
I didn't see how *we all* could've decided anything when I
knew nothing about it. She said there's nothing she can do
if I'm going to continue having Out of Body Experiences.
I was sitting right *there*, in *that* chair and I nodded as if I was
listening, so—as far as *she's* concerned—I was told. I said
so I give up, what's an Oxford Christmas? Nan says Jesus
does a lot of sighing in the Bible because the blokes He

246

hangs out with frustrate Him, but I doubt He sighs more than my mother. After she finished **SIGHING**, she practically screamed at me, "Not **OXFORD**, Janet! **OXFAM**!" I said, "What? You mean Oxfam *the charity shop*?" She said, "**PRECISELY**." The idea is that instead of spending hundreds and hundreds of pounds on pointless presents and tons of food that you don't need (half of which gets thrown out, apparently) and all the other commercial crap associated with Christmas, we're going to give the money we would've spent to Oxfam to help the hungry and oppressed and have a simple dinner and exchange small gifts, preferably ones we made ourselves!!! She might as well have said we were getting a donkey and walking to Bethlehem. I said, "You're joking, right?" She said no. I said but I thought I was getting a new mobe! The MC said not unless she can knit me one, I'm not. I said this was all Buskin' Bob's idea, wasn't it? She said she didn't think the idea that Christmas is about the birth of Christ and not about seeing how much money you can spend originated with Robert. I said it did as far as I was concerned.

SATURDAY 15 DECEMBER

This may be the season of *Peace and Love and Goodwill to All Men* in the rest of the world, but in this house it's all systems as usual. (There certainly isn't any goodwill toward ME!) Got up this morning to find the Mad Cow in one of her less attractive MOODS. Apparently the Abominable Brother asked her to send him the rest of his savings—only it isn't where he said it would be. Of course, she immediately blamed her only daughter! I said that since Justin's South of the Border and therefore probably on drugs, it's unlikely that he remembers *where* he hid his dosh—IF he actually left any behind. She said to pull the other one. I pointed out that as I'd worked my fingers to the bone all summer, I had no motive for taking Geek Boy's money. Rising to her title of Queen of the Nitpickers, the Mad Cow said that I hadn't worked all summer; I'd only worked a few weeks. And she'd never known me to need a motive to spend money. I said I couldn't believe that she was accusing me, the baby girl she'd longed for, of stealing. And she shook the empty jar in my face and said she'd hate to have to dust it for fingerprints. I said it wasn't like I'd nicked it or anything—I'd only borrowed it. She said then I could give it back—**NOW**. Which, of course, I couldn't, could I? I said if he put his money in the bank like normal people, I wouldn't've been tempted. She said she'd lay out the money for him but she's charging me **INTEREST**. I said I didn't think that was showing much Christmas Spirit and she said that taking things that don't belong to you wasn't showing much Christmas Spirit either.

Rang Marcus to see if I could go around to his for Christmas, but turns out his family's going to stay in a lighthouse somewhere off the coast of Scotland till New Year's Day (he doesn't have a clue as to why—neither of his parents has ever shown any interest in the sea). As yet another example of how unpredictable the male of the species can be, Marcus thought the Oxfam Christmas sounded like a brilliant idea (probably because he doesn't have to do it). He said he's pretty fed up with the gross commercialization of Christmas too. He said things are so out of control he wouldn't be surprised if they had Harry Potter advent calendars. What did Harry Potter have to do with Christmas? It was about the coming of Jesus not Harry Potter. Somehow, when Marcus says this kind of thing it isn't as annoying as when Buskin' Bob says it.

I completely agreed. I said did he remember that Christmas when Birds Eye paid for the lights in the West End? At first everybody thought it was meant to be the Dove of Peace swinging over Oxford Street, but turned out it was the Birds Eye logo. So it was actually the Dove of Peas! Marcus thought that was hilarious. He said he'd be *très* relieved if his family decided they should all make their own presents—then he wouldn't have to go shopping. He says shopping takes *years* off your life.

SUNDAY 16 DECEMBER

As much as I like the idea of not having to spend any money on Christmas presents (especially since I'm **IN DEBT**!), I am v busy as per usual and don't see when I'm going to have the time to make anything. Also, I don't know what I *can* make—unless it's a gag for Lucrezia. (I've got that book for Nan, which I reckon is all right since I didn't actually **BUY** it. So that's one down.) I asked Sappho if she had any ideas. She got out this book she bought in that cheap shop in Camden. It tells you what

250

you can make out of stuff you find around the house and is full of things like papier-mâché jewelry boxes, bottle-top earrings, and coasters made of dried macaroni and beans. (You can see why it was sold for pennies—I'm surprised they weren't giving it away.) I pointed out that I'm a *Creative Artist*, not a craftsperson. Sappho couldn't see the difference. She said well, why not knit everybody a scarf (something only a hippie would think of!)? I said I couldn't knit. Ditto crochet. Woodworking, pottery, and metal sculpture are also out. As are candles since the time I poured hot wax all over the cooker. Sappho said, "You're always talking about your poetry—why not write everybody a poem?" I said that was a typical layperson's attitude. I said you don't just sit down and write a poem. Just one poem takes months, not a couple of weeks. Also, you have to be in the mood. Sappho said what about biscuits? I asked if she was offering or just hungry? She said no, really. Why don't I make homemade biscuits? My question was: Why would I want to do that? Apparently I'd want to do that because homemade biscuits are special and a *Gift of Love*. And they don't require Inspiration. I said I didn't see what was so special and *Full of Love* about something you can buy for 59p in Safeway (assuming you're *allowed* in Safeway). Sappho said that was the point, wasn't it? What makes them special is that I make them myself. I can decorate them with colored sugar so they look really Christmassy. She says the cheap shop always has really nice gift boxes and tins for under a quid, so after they eat the biscuits they can still use the container. I said I thought she was forgetting one teensy thing— which is that my culinary skills pretty much start with a cup of tea and end with a hard-boiled egg (I've given up on soft-boiled). Apparently biscuits are dead easy.

MONDAY 17 DECEMBER

Disha's still avoiding me like I have some **MAJOR** communicable disease. She was all over Catriona Hendley at lunch like honey on a spoon. I wish there really was an Aunt K to console me. (I mean, one who isn't **ME**—*oh, physician heal thyself*, right?) I just can't believe that the bus of friendship has moved on without me. Especially over an **AUSTRALIAN** with hairy ears.

TUESDAY 18 DECEMBER

Since I haven't come up with any more ideas on what
inexpensive and easy presents I can make for Christmas in
the Third World, I snuck into the supermarket after school
today to check out the baking section. You wouldn't
believe what they want for this tiny little tub of green or
red sugar! Unless it was hand-dyed by Father Christmas,
it's **ABSOLUTELY OUTRAGEOUS**. And forget the
other stuff like the chocolate bits—you'd think they were
made out of gold and they're not even made out of
chocolate! (I can't stop reading labels now—no matter
how hard I try.) Was on my way back to Green Army
Headquarters when who should I see with her arms loaded
with shopping but **SKY**?!! (I've always said there's
NOTHING spiritual about her, haven't I?) I believe
I was divinely inspired because, instead of turning right
around and acting like I hadn't seen her, I actually accosted
her. Blah blah blah . . . How are you . . . ? Blah blah
blah . . . Been Christmas shopping . . . ? Blah blah blah . . .
It was all pretty mindless and excruciatingly boring. But
then Sky said something about Durango and I said (and
this is where *Divine Inspiration* comes in), "Oh, are you

still working there? I thought Disha said you'd left." Sky wanted to know who Disha was. I said, "You know, Ethan's girlfriend. She's my best mate—he met her through me." That was the moment when I finally understood why Justin always lugs a camera around with him. Oh, how I wish I could've photographed Sky's face when I said those magic words "Ethan's girlfriend." Not that I'm likely to ever forget it, of course, but it'd be nice to show people. Sky wanted to know what I was on about. She said, "I'M ETHAN'S GIRLFRIEND." I pretended to be all flustered and shocked (acting is *definitely* another of the many career possibilities open to me). I said I thought they hardly knew each other, and she said they kept quiet about it at work because of Saduki and all his rules. I was still stammering apologies and muttering about me and my big mouth as Sky stalked off with Blood in Her Eye! It is definitely the season to be jolly! I was half tempted to get David and Marcus and race around to Durango to watch the fireworks.

WEDNESDAY 19 DECEMBER

(There is a Father Christmas!!!)

I was having an absolutely fascinating conversation with
Sappho tonight about **Birthing Horror Stories** (thirty days in
labor . . . twenty-pound babies . . . quadruplets two days
apart . . . the sorts of things that make a young girl long to
be pregnant) when the doorbell rang. Normally I'm not
that eager to drag myself all the way down the hall to find
out it's a family of Jehovah's Witnesses or some bloke
selling tea towels, but I was pretty worn out by Sappho's
tales of **suffering and pain** (you'd think having a baby would
be easy—I mean, **EVERYTHING** does it; how can
it be so hard?). You can imagine my **SHOCK** and
SURPRISE when I opened the door to find **DISHA
PASKI** standing there! She was wearing the orange top I
gave her and had a package wrapped in silver paper with a
purple ribbon around it, and she was crying. I said well, it
was nice that she was so glad to see me. She said she was
sorry for everything, especially for **DOUBTING ME**.
She met Ethan tonight and Sky suddenly jumped out from
behind a building and let rip. Disha said she couldn't

believe that all this time Ethan was two-timing her by two-timing Sky. It really is true that we're at the mercy of our feelings. Here was my chance to be v sarky and get even, and what did I do? I STARTED CRYING TOO!!!
I said I was sorry for not being more sensitive (though I don't know how I could have been when she never told ME anything!). Disha said I was right about Ethan's jealousy but she hadn't known how to handle it. Being a rabid feminist, Sappho doesn't usually have any time for weeping women, so it must be her impending motherhood that's changed her because Disha and I weren't halfway down the hall before she came shuffling out of the kitchen wanting to know what was wrong. I said nothing; everything was all right now. Sappho offered to make us tea! (Which means it truly is the *Season of Miracles*!!!)

THURSDAY 20 DECEMBER

Buskin' Bob has returned from saving Malaysia with a new hat (batik) and a tan. He was in the kitchen POPPING CORN when I got back from Disha's this afternoon.

I said he did know you can buy it in bags already buttered and salted, didn't he? And he said it wasn't for eating; it was for stringing. I said **PARDON**? He said strings of popcorn are much nicer than environmentally unfriendly tinsel on the tree. If you ask me, this is a matter of personal taste. I like tinsel and I don't care if takes three billion years to decompose either. To add insult to aesthetic injury, he expected **ME** to do the stringing! I said I had a previous engagement and went over to Marcus's.

FRIDAY 21 DECEMBER

Today's the winter solstice, which is Sappho's Big Holiday. She turned on all the fairy lights that are still up from my party and it looked well cool. (That was the highlight.) Next Sappho put on a CD of some pagans chanting. Then she lit some incense and candles and read a poem about a tree, and then we had sweet cider and oatcakes. That was about it really. (You can understand why people turned to Christianity, can't you? The food and the music are très, très better.) Since the solstice isn't over-commercialized like

Christmas, Sappho bought our presents. I got a postcard book of Frida Kahlo paintings (because I *once* mentioned her to Sappho). I was hoping for another diary. Was saved having to pretend to be too enthusiastic because the incense made Sappho nauseous and she wobbled off to the loo as soon as she gave out her gifts, and spent the rest of the night vomiting. [Note to self: Did the Virgin Mary have to go through this?]

SATURDAY 22 DECEMBER

The MC had a party to go to tonight and Sappho was beached on the sofa, so I decided it was a good time for biscuit making. I'd already picked my recipe (Basic Sugar Cookies). First I had to dye the sugar for the tops with food coloring. Then I had to melt the margarine to get it soft enough to mix with the flour. After that, I discovered that we were right out of vanilla flavoring, so I had to use a dollop of the Christmas sherry instead. And then I had to **ROLL OUT** the dough, which is v time-consuming and not as easy as it sounds. The first lot stuck to the counter.

The second lot stuck to the table. Asked Sappho, who said you're meant to roll it on a floured surface. I said well, why didn't it say that? And she said it did. Had to move all the small appliances to the floor to make enough room on the counter. And something went horribly wrong with the colored sugar. First of all, the colors weren't too brilliant. Also, it turned into a paste! I'd been at it for hours, so I wasn't about to do it all over again. Spread it on with a knife. Put the baking sheets in the oven, set the timer, and went to take a quick shower since I was **COVERED** in flour. When I came out of the bathroom the flat was filled with smoke, the alarm was shrieking away, and Sappho was hanging out of the back door being sick in the garden. (I don't know why they call it Morning Sickness; she does it morning, noon, and night!) The MC was at the sink with a tea towel across her face looking v unfestive. Of course, she blamed **ME**! She wanted to know what I was trying to do—**BURN THE HOUSE DOWN**? I said I was making my Christmas presents, wasn't I? **WHICH WASN'T MY IDEA**. I'm perfectly happy to have a commercialized and materialistic Christmas like everybody else. Also, now I'm going to end up giving everyone empty boxes.

SUNDAY 23 DECEMBER

The gods of burnt biscuits left me no choice—I've had to give in and buy presents for my *extraordinarily extended* family. I reckoned that as long as I got really inexpensive little things, I couldn't be accused of rampant materialism or contributing to the commercial bloodbath that is Christmas. Disha went with me to the cheap shop beloved of Sappho. (Not only is it cheap, but a lot of the stuff comes from China or somewhere like that. According to Robert, most of it is handmade by blind prisoners and orphans. So, if you ask me, that means it's v close to being homemade.) It was brilliant. I got something for **EVERYONE** (even Sappho's baby). And for a lot less than a T-shirt! Was so chuffed I treated Disha to lunch in the West End so we could do some shopping for ourselves while we were out. Waiting for the bus is usually *très* boring and irksome, but today it was **DISGUSTING** as well. There was **VOMIT** at every stop. D said that's how you know it's Christmas—that and the lights and the manger, etc. We had a brilliant time. Everybody always bangs on about how **IMPORTANT** friendship is, but it's true! It's only now the real Disha Paski has reclaimed her body that I realize how much I missed her while she was the **Zombie of Love**. Disha says the same. She says being in *Love* was très exciting and all, but now that it's over, she wonders what it was really about. She says she was out of her mind most of the time because of Ethan's jealousy. You won't believe this—she ACTUALLY wrote to Aunt K!! Disha was But I Love Him! She said Aunt K was right (of course!) but at the time Disha thought she was v offhand and dismissive. I said I didn't think that was true at all. I said that Aunt K was just demonstrating her incredible knowledge of human behavior and she should've listened to her. Nearly got into another fight! (Disha's still très defensive.) D said Aunt K may be right NOW, but at the time Disha didn't realize what a deceitful creep Ethan was; she thought he was the *Love of Her Life*. I said so Love Is Blind. Disha said and deaf and dumb as well.

Got back to find that Robert and the Deadly Duo had arrived. The MC made me drag the tree in from the garden, of course, while she and London's Answer to Bob Dylan sat around singing about holly and ivy and drinking environmentally-friendly mulled wine! Marcella wouldn't help, because: (a) she didn't want to get dirty; (b) she'd just done her nails; and (c) she prefers artificial trees

(I wonder if it's possible that **NEITHER** of them are actually Buskin' Bob's). Perverse as always, Lucrezia **INSISTED** on helping, then got a microscopic needle from the tree stuck in her hand and practically had to be hospitalized! Was exhausted by the time we got it inside. Since the fairy lights are still up and it doesn't look like anyone's going to take them down, we at least didn't have to go through the drama of putting them on the tree. Marcella doesn't like our ornaments, and Lucrezia was still **SUFFERING UNSILENTLY**, so I got volunteered to do the decorating while Buskin' Bob went off to get the popcorn. That's when he discovered we have mice (or possibly rats—something that likes popcorn, anyway). The MC came after me like a nuclear warhead! She was all atwitter because in searching for mouse holes she found the dishes I put away in the broom cupboard and is holding them responsible for the **INFESTATION**. (Shows how much she cleans up—that was **AGES** ago! And she says I'm a lazy cow!) Blah blah blah . . . She actually stood next to me while I washed them, with her arms folded across her chest! I said you better watch out or your face will stay like that. Let me assure you that having a boyfriend has done nothing for her sense of humor!

162

*   *   *

More trauma while the MC and the Eco Warrior continued to scour the kitchen for mouse holes. Lucrezia and Marcella locked themselves in the bathroom for safety from the rodents of London. Of course, it was Cinderella Bandry who had to race to Woolies for tinsel. What would any of them do without me?

Asked Marcella why she came here, to the Third World, for Christmas when she could've stayed at home with her artificial tree. She said because the Actress and the Entrepreneur have gone on a cruise. Also, she doesn't mind about no presents, food, crackers, or other festivities because they celebrated early at her mum's, so she got all the stuff she wanted and they even let her have a glass of champagne. Here, if she wants a glass of water she'll probably have to go to the well for it.

CHRISTMAS EVE

Sigmund had to fetch Nan this morning. I said I'd be happy
to go with him and do the driving, but he **REFUSED**.
He said he thought Nan was way too old to survive a
journey with **ME**, even if she was a spy in the war. I went
along for the ride anyway (he wouldn't even let me drive
going, on the grounds that he's too close to seeing another
year in to risk it!). Even if it meant being squashed in the
back with Nan's bags, it was better than staying at home as
Robert had everyone stringing cranberries (apparently not
on the mouse menu) instead of the popcorn. I noticed that
one of Nan's bags was filled up with placards. I said what's
this, have you got a job advertising the January sales?
Apparently there's a Peace Vigil tonight. I said Christmas
Eve's an odd time to have a demonstration—everybody's
going to be at parties or getting drunk or whatever. Nan
says Christmas is peace. Sigmund said tell that to the
Vietnamese (whose present from President Nixon was to
have Hanoi flattened by bombs, apparently). Of course, as
soon as the Mad Cow clapped eyes on the placards, she
decreed that I should go to Parliament Square with Nan (it's
obvious that the MC was an Absolute Monarch in a former

life and I was a serf). I said you mean that while everybody else in the world is watching television and eating chocolates, I'm going to be standing in the rain with Nan, trying to keep my candle from going out? The MC said that was precisely what she meant. D was already off visiting the family, but Marcus isn't leaving town till the morning so I decided to see if he'd come with me. If you asked most boys whether they wanted to spend Christmas Eve standing in the cold and the rain with a bunch of fanatical Christians, they'd say no, right off. But not Marcus. Artists are meant to be moody and temperamental, but even though Marcus is an excellent painter (Mr. Belakis says he's a dead-cert for Saint Martin's), he has a v patient and flexible nature—more like a fisherman than a *Creative Spirit*. Marcus said of course he'd come. He said it was better than watching *Toy Story* again—and he always likes to do new things. So off we went on the bus with Nan and her placards. There were a few more people down at Parliament Square than there were in the manger in Bethlehem—but not many. (And not a shepherd or king in sight!) My first thought was that they must all be homeless, but it turned out most of them were Quakers. Nan made straight for this old geezer with a golden lab. It was wearing a sign that said

LET LOOSE THE DOGS OF PEACE. The old geezer was wearing a bowler hat and carrying an umbrella with a peace symbol painted on it. If you ask me, he looked like one of those blokes who walk around with signs saying that the world's about to end, so I tried to stop her, but it turned out he's the **PRIEST** that runs Nan's Jesus group, the Very Reverend Jerym Noad. The dog's name is Luke. Both of them seemed pretty pleased to see Nan (which must make a nice change for her). Nan latched onto them and more or less forgot about me and Marcus. Marcus said it looked like my gran's got a beau. I said he must be mad. My nan hasn't dated since the war. Also, she's **WAY** too old for that sort of thing. Marcus said well, they seemed pretty close, and I said that was because she was sharing his umbrella. Anyway, for a few hours we just stood around trying to keep our candles from going out (as predicted by Janet Bandry!). Then a couple of people started singing "O Holy Night" and then a few more joined in until everybody was singing—even one of the coppers! It was like being in church—except for the rain and the fact that nobody was just *pretending* to sing; they were all belting it out like they really wanted God to hear them (or possibly the Prime Minister, though you can bet he wasn't hanging around

Parliament on Christmas Eve). I moved closer to Marcus because it was cold, etc., and he put his arm around me. It really is true that you **NEVER** really know what's going to happen next. I turned to Marcus to say that I could murder a hot cup of tea and (wait for it!) . . . **HE KISSED ME**!!! Right there in front of Big Ben! I said, "What's that for?" He said, "It's Christmas," and held up a piece of mistletoe he'd brought with him. So I kissed him back.

CHRISTMAS DAY

Unless I go senile like my mother, as I get older I'm going to remember this Christmas for the rest of my life. I couldn't fall asleep because I could still hear everyone singing at the *Vigil* in my head. Also kept thinking about Marcus kissing me in front of Big Ben. (Is this the start of *Something*? Or is it the end of a *Beautiful Friendship*? If we start going out, will we hate each other by the spring? If we don't hate each other and end up getting married—after my career as whatever is established—will our children all have one eyebrow too?) I was finally sort of drifting off when I heard someone stumbling about in the hall. (The bulb went out ages ago, but as per usual the MC's too lazy to do anything about it. Not only is Love blind, but it wants everyone else to be blind as well.) I ruled out Father Christmas straight away. Then I ruled out the Mad Cow, Sigmund, and Robert because I could hear them all snoring (it's like sleeping with hogs, I swear!). I also ruled out Sappho (wrong direction, she'd be heading for the loo) and Lucrezia and Marcella (because I could see them). I reckoned it must be Nan, because everyone knows that old people are too close to death to sleep much. So I got up and tiptoed out of my room in case she was going to make a cup of tea. Nan likes me well enough (I am her only granddaughter, after all), but she's never been exactly overjoyed to see me before. "Praise the Lord!" cried Nan. "Janet, I need your help!" I said for what? To make tea? She said to ring for an ambulance—she had to get back to Sappho because the baby was coming. Being Nan, I wasn't sure what baby she was talking about. I mean, it could've been the Baby Jesus. (Also, it was très **LATE** and I was shattered.) Nan wanted to know how many babies I thought we were expecting and I said you mean *Sappho's* baby? It's coming here? *Now?* Nan said it probably wanted to be near its mother. I said wouldn't it be faster to get Sigmund to drive her to the hospital and Nan said Mary may have ridden on a donkey, but there was no way Sappho was going to the hospital in the Mini. Making phone calls is one of my natural talents, so I raced to the kitchen and rang the hospital. Then I went to tell Nan the ambulance would be here in probably less than an hour. Sappho was on the bed. (She wasn't screaming the way women having babies on telly do, which I put down to the fact that she's a rabid feminist and doesn't like to seem weak or girly.) I've never seen anyone look pale AND flushed at the same time before. She looked like she'd just run ten miles. Except that her legs were wide open! (I couldn't look! I've seen someone giving birth on telly, but it's not the same as in your own home with a blood relative!) Nan said that less than an hour was probably a bit too late. The baby was coming right this minute! I said but doesn't someone have to deliver it? I didn't think they could just come on their own. Nan said she was an experienced midwife (is there no end to this woman's talents?). She said she delivered many a baby in the war. (I'm going to have to check in the library and see if what I was told in school was wrong and it was Nan who won World War II!) She told me to go and boil water (I still don't know **WHY**!). Sappho yelled at me to ring Mags. So I raced off to boil water and ring Mags. When I got back from that, a scene of **gory horror** met my eyes. Nan was pulling this bloody, goppy-looking thing out of my aunt! [Note to self: In the story of the Nativity, there is **NO** mention of blood or goo or anything like that. Mary always looks like she got the baby in the market.] "Push!" ordered Nan, and Sappho (who usually won't do anything anyone tells her to) pushed. **IT WAS SO GROSS**. I know birth's meant to be a miracle and this brilliant thing, etc., but all I could think was, what a mess! And it didn't even look like a baby. Not a human baby at any rate. (Here is **ABSOLUTE PROOF** that not all babies are beautiful— it looks like a pig!) Comandante Rose Bandry said to stop being stupid and go and wake my parents. By the time the ambulance finally turned up, we were all in the kitchen having tea, even Sappho and the Piglet. Sappho's naming it Germaine after that writer who's always on the box giving her opinion on everything. I said she did realize everyone would call her Germ, didn't she (which, if you ask me, is putting an unreasonable burden on a child that's already off to a bad start)? But Sappho is oblivious to things like peer pressure. Having got the birthing bit over with, Sappho

went straight back to Nobody Tells **ME** What to Do mode
and refused to go to the hospital on the grounds that it was
like going to a restaurant after you'd eaten dinner. Was just
thinking of going back to bed when Nan's priest and his
dog rolled up! (See what I mean about old people and
sleep? It was practically dawn!) I asked Nan what **THEY**
were doing here and she said they'd come to share the
fatted lentil loaf with us. She said she thought it was time
Jerym met everybody. I said, "And why's that, then?" Nan
got all coy (which is a sight I've never seen before, believe
me!) and said, "Because he's more or less part of the family,
isn't he?" I said, "Nobody told **ME**." She said many are
called but they don't all come. If you ask me, this family's
getting way too big. We're going to have to move in with
the Queen at the rate we're going! (Or I'm going to have to
get a bigger canvas!) It wasn't like spending Christmas with
anyone normal, but it wasn't completely **DREADFUL**
either. The food was all right. The presents aren't going to
make Jennifer Lopez wish she was part of our family, but
they were all right too. Buskin' Bob wrote me a song called
"Planet Janet in Orbit" (which was actually funny—esp. if
you're not **ME**). The MC made me a photo album with
pictures in it of me when I was little (which was touching

in a sad and bittersweet way—and useful for my portrait).
Nan knitted me this *très* cool jumper that she copied from a
magazine. Lucrezia made me a bookmark with my name on
it, and Marcella decorated a cigar box with glitter and
sequins and a picture of me, her, and the **Little Horror** in the
rain in Wales (which I suppose I can incorporate into my
art project, since it looks like I really am stuck with them)
for me to keep jewelry in. And Sigmund broke all the rules
and bought me ten lessons with a proper driving school
because he said his nerves really couldn't take any more.
(And mine could?) Everybody **LOVED** my gifts.
(Especially Nan! She said she'd been wanting to read that
book. Robert said it was really good; he had a copy himself.
Didn't I say he'd never know?) Of course, after we ate, we
had to sit around singing for a few hours. I didn't mind it
as much as usual, but I think that was because Jerym
contributed champagne to the dinner. (I notice Robert
didn't tell him he could've fed some child in Africa for six
months on what that cost!) Then we had to take pictures so
that in years to come we'll think we had a brilliant time.
Not only did I have to pose with the Deadly Duo but I had
the Piglet on my lap as well. (She pissed all over me.)

BOXING DAY

Went around to Disha's to get away from all the singing
and crying at our house. Told her about Christmas Eve and
she **WAS ASTOUNDED!** She said you really kissed
him back? I said twice. Disha wanted to know if that was
it then and Marcus and I are officially an item. I said I've
been giving it **TONS** of thought (which I have—when
it's quiet enough in the **House of Horror** to think). I said I'd
decided that when he gets back, I'm going to tell him that
I thought we both got swept away in the moment with
the singing and the rain and the clock and all and that it
wouldn't be a good idea to add snogging to our personal
itinerary. She said that's v mature of me. I said I know.

THURSDAY 27 DECEMBER

Disha came over to meet the Piglet today. D thinks she's
cute. I said she's been hitting the Christmas eggnog too
hard. The Piglet's only cute if you're comparing her to the
rest of the barnyard. Showed Disha my Oxfam Christmas

273

presents. She said I did v well. At least I didn't get any bath gel or anything like that (she got three bottles of gel, two of foaming bubbles, and four lots of oil balls!). Disha thinks it's cool to have things **MADE** for you. It shows people are really thinking about you. I said they could think about me in any major department store as well.

FRIDAY 28 DECEMBER

Went with D to exchange some of her Christmas toiletries today. Lila was in the Body Shop, exchanging some stuff she'd been given. I said, "You're still not speaking to the Hendley even in this season of goodwill?" She said she can't speak to her because she's in Bali. I said, "**SHE'S WHAT**? **ANOTHER HOLIDAY**?" Lila said not exactly. She said Catriona *Fell in Love* with a waiter in the hotel where she stayed in the summer and has run off to be with him. Disha and I were both pretty **GOBSMACKED**. But I could see some good news for me personally in all this. I said so she's not coming back to school in the New Year? **WHAT A SHAME**. Lila said she'll be back. The parent Hendleys have gone after her. I said well, you kept pretty quiet about this. Lila said she'd been **SWORN TO SECRECY**. I said fancy the Hendley falling for a Balinese waiter! Lila said he was Australian. I said well, at least we know it isn't Ethan, and Disha and I cracked up in a major way. Lila said she didn't see what was so funny.

MONDAY 31 DECEMBER

Was just getting ready to go over to Disha's for New Year's Eve (it's becoming our tradition!) when the phone rang. It was Marcus. He said he would've rung me sooner but there's no phone in the lighthouse and this was the first chance he'd had. He wanted to know if I'd been thinking about **US**. I said a bit. He said he hadn't been able to put Christmas Eve out of his mind. He says it was the best night of his life! And I must know how much he likes me since he's never tried to hide his feelings. He said he thought we should go out properly. He wanted to know if that was what I thought too. I surprised myself by saying yes.

TUESDAY 1 JANUARY

ANOTHER NEW YEAR BEGINS! (I'm not sure whether I should rush out to greet it or duck for cover!) Disha and I talked so much last night that midnight came and went before we even noticed! We certainly had QUITE A YEAR!!! D said that even though there was a certain amount of **emotional turmoil** and **pain and suffering**, she actually found it all sort of exciting. She said at least we've started to really live. I agreed. I said but I thought that, all things considered, it was just as well we'd jacked in the Dark Phase, since Life is dark enough without having to egg it on.

GLOSSARY

59P 59 pence (Pence are the smallest denomination of money in the U.K., similar to U.S. pennies.)

999 U.K. equivalent of 911

A-LEVEL ENGLISH advanced-level exam in English, usually taken at age 18

ADVERT advertisement

AUBERGINE eggplant

BANGING ON talking endlessly

BIG BEN nickname of the Great Bell of Westminster, the hour bell of the Great Clock, hanging in the Clock Tower of the Houses of Parliament

BIN trash can

BISCUITS cookies

BLACKPOOL a seaside resort in northwest England

BLOKES men/boys

BLOODY very; used as an all-purpose intensifier

BOG ROLL toilet paper

BOMB large sum of money

BOOT trunk of a car

BOTTLE BANK a bottle recycling bin

BORSTAL BOYS juvenile delinquents (Borstal was a juvenile detention center.)

BOX, THE television

BOXING DAY the day after Christmas, a public holiday

BRILLIANT very good, excellent

BUDGIE POO parakeet poo

BUSKIN' performing on the street

CAMDEN MARKET a famous street market in north London; pretty much the goth capital of the world

CAPITAL FM a radio station

CAR PARK parking lot

CARRIER BAG plastic shopping bag

CHANNEL, THE the English Channel; body of water separating England from France

CHEEKY impudent, saucy

CHEESED OFF irritated, annoyed

CHEMIST pharmacy

CHILD-MINDER babysitter

CHILL ME OUT relax me

CHIPS french fries

CHUFFED pleased

CLAPHAM an area of south London

COLOR SUPPLEMENT the magazine that comes with the Saturday or Sunday newspaper

COMBATS fatigues

COOKER stove

CRACKER a Christmas party favor that gives a satisfying bang when you open it and contains a tissue-paper crown and other trinkets

CRISPS potato chips

CUPBOARD closet

CUPPA cup of tea

DEAD-CERT absolute certainty, sure thing

DEMO political demonstration

DOLLIS HILL a quiet residential section of London

DOSH money

ESSO gas station chain

FAIRY LIGHTS Christmas lights

FAG cigarette

FANCY have a crush on; like or desire

FÊTE fair

FLASH flashy, ostentatious

FLAT apartment

FORM prison record

GARDEN yard

GENTS men's room

GCSEs General Certificate of Secondary Education exams, usually taken at age 16

GINORMOUS made-up word; amalgamation of gigantic and enormous; very big

GM genetically modified

GOBSMACKED astounded

GREENGROCER retail seller of fresh fruits and vegetables

GUY FAWKES an English conspirator and member of the 1604 Gunpowder Plot, aimed at blowing up Parliament; Guy Fawkes Day is observed annually in England with bonfires, fireworks, and parties

HALF-TERM one-week midsemester vacation

HAMPSTEAD HEATH heath (open tract of uncultivated land) in north London

HAVE A LIE-IN sleep in; stay in bed later than usual

HEAD headmaster, principal

HERS, HIS her place, his place

HIGH STREET Main Street; the main road in a town

HOLIDAY, HOLIDAYS vacation

INDUSTRIAL ESTATE industrial park

IN PRETTY GOOD NICK in good condition

JACK IN quit

JUBILEE, QUEEN'S FIRST anniversary of the coronation

JUMPER sweater

KILBURN area below Dollis Hill, features cafés and inexpensive shops

KING'S CROSS major train station

KIP sleep

KNICKERS underpants

LAY OUT give, loan

LIFT elevator

LOO toilet, lavatory

MAD crazy

MARKS AND SPARKS Marks & Spencer, a British clothing and grocery store

MARMITE a savory spread made from yeast

MATES friends

MATHS math

MIND babysit

MOBE mobile phone/cell phone

NAPPIES diapers

NATTER chat

NICKED arrested; stolen

NOTHING FOR IT nothing else to do

OFFING, IN THE a possibility

ON ABOUT talking about

ON TOP FORM in good form

OURS our place

OXFAM charitable organization based in the U.K.; runs shops selling secondhand clothes and goods as well as fair-trade products made in developing countries

PARLIAMENT SQUARE square outside of Parliament (home of U.K. national legislature); frequent site of demonstrations

PETROL gas

PICCADILLY CIRCUS busy junction of five streets in London, the U.K. equivalent of Times Square

PISSING DOWN raining heavily

PLAITED braided

POST mail

POST OFFICE TOWER British Telecom communications tower, a London landmark

POT NOODLE plastic cup of instant noodles

POUND basic monetary unit of the United Kingdom

PRIMARY elementary school

PRIME MINISTER leader of the party with the majority in the House of Commons

QUID pound(s); five hundred quid is equivalent to almost one thousand dollars

RAC Royal Automobile Club; a road service, like AAA in the U.S.

RANG called

REVISE study

ROUNDABOUT traffic rotary

ROW, ROWING argument, arguing

SAFEWAY grocery store chain

SALT CELLAR saltshaker

SARKY sarcastic

SARNIES sandwiches

SAS Special Air Service

SHATTERED exhausted

SKIP Dumpster

SNOGGING kissing passionately; making out

SODS pains in the butt

SOLICITOR lawyer

SPANNER wrench

SPOTS acne

ST. MARTIN'S prestigious art school

SWANNING AROUND swaggering

TAKE-AWAY takeout

TEA COSY padded cloth covering to keep a teapot warm

TELLY television

TERM school semester

THOMAS COOK a travel agency

THORPE PARK an amusement park

TILL GONE MIDNIGHT after midnight

TIN tin can

TOP SHOP a chain of fashionable, affordable clothing stores

TRAINERS sneakers

TRAINSPOTTING an obsessive hobby that involves watching trains and recording their types, names, and numbers; often used as an example of an extremely boring activity

TROLLEY shopping cart

TUBE London subway

V very

V&A Victoria and Albert Museum

WARDROBE external closet

WELL very

WELLIES Wellingtons; high, waterproof rubber boots

WEST END shopping and entertainment district of central London

WHACKED exhausted

WHOLEMEAL whole wheat

WINDSCREEN windshield

WOMBLE character featured in a series of children's books and, later, a television show; Wombles are fantastical creatures who live on Wimbledon Common.

WOOLIE'S affectionate term for Woolworth's, a chain of five-and-dime stores that no longer operates in the U.S. but is still in business in the U.K.

YEAR 7S students in their first year of secondary school, for ages 11 to 12